the whistle

the whistle

valerie rolfe lupini

Red Deer PRESS

Published by
Red Deer Press
Trailer C
2500 University Drive N.W.
Calgary Alberta Canada T2N 1N4
www.reddeerpress.com

Credits
Edited for the Press by Peter Carver
Copyedited by Lee Shenkman
Cover and text design by Erin Woodward
Cover image courtesy Masterfile and the Glenbow Archives NA–2883.6
Printed and bound in Canada by Friesens for Red Deer Press

Acknowledgments
Financial support provided by the Canada Council, the Government of Canada
through the Book Publishing Industry Development Program (BPIDP), the
Alberta Foundation for the Arts, a beneficiary of the Lottery Fund of the
Government of Alberta, and the University of Calgary.

THE CANADA COUNCIL | LE CONSEIL DES ARTS
FOR THE ARTS | DU CANADA
SINCE 1957 | DEPUIS 1957

National Library of Canada Cataloguing in Publication
Rolfe Lupini, Valerie, 1960–
The whistle / Valerie Rolfe Lupini.
ISBN 0-88995-314-7
I. Title.
PS8585.O3965W49 2005   jC813'.54   C2005-901972-7

Dedicated with love to Jesse, Elliot and Peter,

and to the memory of my grandparents,

Leslie and Basil Rolfe

Kathleen and Wyndham Madden

Prologue

Humphrey Mills fell. He'd been throwing a tennis ball out to sea for over half an hour in an effort to tire his dog Jester. Making his way up the stone stairs from the beach, he miscalculated a step and tripped. He heard the tibia crack.

After examining his leg and trying unsuccessfully to stand upright, the old man rolled awkwardly onto his back and began to heave himself, little by little, toward the house. His arms and right leg ached with the strain of it, while the injured limb slid and jostled along the ground. By the time he'd dragged himself to the hall table and dialed 911, Humphrey Mills was in excruciating pain. When the ambulance arrived, he lay unconscious on the carpet, the dog wedged against his side.

Chapter One

"I hope the key is in the same place," said Nora Devon as she tipped back a ceramic pot on the porch to look.

"It's all wormy under there." Mary knelt down and peered under the pot.

"Can you see it?"

"Don't let go," said Mary as she reached her hand underneath and unearthed the key to the front door. *"Voila!"*

"Well done." Mary's mum dusted off her jeans, and unlocked the front door.

Mary stepped inside. The front hall was as she remembered it—warm, white, paneled walls and a thick, wool Persian carpet. A small desk with a telephone and directory stood in one corner, while the stairs occupied the other. Mary hadn't been in this house for five years; yet it had an appealing familiarity. It felt like Grandad.

"Would you please give me a hand?" Mary's mum called from the driveway. "How about bringing in your suitcase?"

Mary ran outside to where the taxi driver had unloaded their belongings. She gathered up her jacket and bag, her backpack and book, and dumped them at the foot of the stairs. As she did so, she noticed on the stair landing a portrait of a young man.

"Who's he again?" asked Mary.

Nora Devon put her suitcase beside Mary's. "Rudyard Mills, your great grandfather."

"Oh, yeah." Mary twirled the end of her braid. "He doesn't look like Grandad."

"No," said Mary's mother. "He doesn't much." She rubbed the small of her back. "But your Grandad is an old man now and looked a lot different when he was younger."

They trudged up the stairs and into the pretty guest room with matching twin beds divided by a night table.

Mary plunked herself down on one of the beds, smoothing her hands over the quilted pink cover. "I remember these quilts."

"Do you?"

"I used to lure Jester up here with a cookie and play with him."

"You didn't."

Mary grinned. "I did."

"How did you manage that?"

"When Grandad took his nap, I'd go to the kitchen and take Jester by his collar and bring him upstairs. He loved it. He went nuts up here! He'd chase me all around the room and we'd lie on the bed together."

Mary's mum looked aghast. "You let him up on the bed?"

"*In* the bed, too, with his head on my pillow."

"Mary!"

"Mum!"

"You know that Grandad wouldn't approve."

"Jester approved." Mary stretched out on the bed, her hands behind her head. "I felt sorry for him. He loved coming up here. He even loved it when I dressed him up."

"Dressed him up?" Mum put the suitcase in the closet.

"In my dressing gown and slippers, bathing suit and goggles, biggish T-shirts. He looked great. Especially in sunglasses. But shorts were impossible. His tail was awkward."

"Grandad would have a fit if he knew. Jester's been trained as a hunting dog."

"Hunting shmunting. It's cruel."

Mary's mum sat on the bed across from her daughter. "He's never hunted as an adult. It's just that he's trained his dogs this way—to be obedient and unspoiled."

Mary rolled onto her side. "Can you ask Grandad if we can get Jester from the Kellys? I can take care of him and he'll be happier in his own house."

"I dare say."

"Dare say yes or dare say no?"

Mum hung a coat in the closet. "I'm too tired to think about that now. I really want to get to the hospital to see Grandad."

Mary looked pained.

"I won't be long," said Mum. "I'm sure he won't be up for much of a visit." She put her cosmetic bag in the bathroom. "That reminds me . . . "

Mary followed her mother down the carpeted hallway to her grandfather's bedroom. Tidy and mannish, it had a well-worn carpet, bed, dresser, tie rack, and overstuffed armchair. When Mary's mum went into Grandad's bathroom to collect a few things, Mary switched on a lamp.

She was startled. Almost every inch of the dresser's surface was taken up with the crafts, gifts, paintings, and photos that Mary had sent him over the years. The paintings were taped to the wall as a backdrop for the framed photos of herself playing soccer, playing the fiddle, showing off Doris, her cat, and one of her on her fifth birthday. Origami pieces she'd sent him carefully wrapped in a shoe box—a crane, a pencil, a tree, two lily pads and a frog—were interspersed among these photos. Such a colorful display compared to the far right-hand side of the dresser, where a collection of black-and-white photographs stood corralled under the light of the lamp. Mary leaned closer to inspect the faces.

"This must be Granny and Grandad when they were young," said Mary.

Mum walked out of the bathroom with a toothbrush and paste. "Probably before they were married."

"And these two?"

"That's Rudyard Mills again, and his wife—your great grandmother, Louise."

"She's so pretty."

Mum looked closer. "She was, wasn't she?"

"He looks too serious."

Mary's mum put the toothbrush and paste in a plastic bag. "Maybe he didn't like his picture being taken." She opened a dresser drawer and pulled out underwear and socks. "Maybe they'd just had a great, whopping argument."

"He must've lost," Mary scanned the other photos. "Now this is weird!" she exclaimed. "That kid, there, the one beside the boy. She looks like me." Mary looked at Mum.

Nora Devon squinted. "That's Mary. And she does look like you. Same nose or something."

"The one you named me after?"

"The one we named you after." Mum slid a pair of slippers into another bag and headed toward the bedroom door.

"I'm glad her name wasn't Ernestine." Mary smiled.

"We *wouldn't* have named you Ernestine." Mary's mum took off her glasses and polished the lenses on her shirt. "Or Myrtle or Beryl." She put them back on her face. "We liked the name *and* Mary was Grandad's favorite sister."

"Where is she now?"

"Up island in a place called Tofino. She lives with her daughter." Nora Devon looked at Mary who was staring so keenly at the photo. "I guess that the down side of living back east is that you sort of miss out on knowing about the family out west. You probably know more about Dad's relatives than mine. The relations out here must seem very confusing."

Mary followed her mother back down the hallway. "Why can't I come to the hospital?"

"It's too soon, dear. Grandad's in intensive care; he'll be very, very tired. I think I should go quietly alone."

"I can be quiet."

"I don't even know if two people are allowed in the room."

Mary pushed her hands into her jeans pockets. "We could take turns."

Mum put everything down on the guest bed and gave her daughter a hug. "Why are you being so persistent?"

"I just *really* want to see Grandad," she implored. "I want to give him the card I made and I don't want to stay in this house by myself right now."

Mary's mum sighed, scooped up the belongings, and headed downstairs. Mary followed. They passed the portrait of Rudyard Mills on the stairway landing. Mum disappeared into the kitchen; and though Mary wanted to follow her, to explore the old house as she once had, she felt peculiarly drawn to the portrait.

"Oil," Mary whispered, as though she was convincing herself that this was simply a painting, because, as she stood before it, she felt a probing warmth.

She was willing herself to be brave and to look this man, her great grandfather, directly in the eye. His mouth was terse, there were flecks of orange on his cheek, and she wondered whether the light had really danced there or the artist had added it for contrast as she had been taught to do on occasion. She was stalling as her eyes caught the sharp angle of his nose, his auburn mustache, and then the liquidity of his eyes. He seemed to be intently staring at her, though Mary understood that this was illusion, as she'd been taught. Yet his eyes had a depth that seemed greater than the pasty oils and canvas.

"You are just a painting," she whispered.

"Mary?" Mum stood at the foot of the stairs with her shoes on and purse slung over her shoulder. "Did you say something?"

Chapter Two

Mary looked at her mother. "Didn't you tell me that Granny saw a ghost once?"

"In England." She put her hand on the banister.

"And ghosts only live in the UK?"

Nora Devon laughed. "It was at a very old English inn and, according to my mother, the ghost was just sitting in a chair beside her bed—perfectly harmless."

"This house is old."

"That doesn't mean every old house has a ghost." She adjusted her glasses on her nose. "I'm off."

"I want to come."

"You can't."

Mary put on her runners. "I want to."

"Oh, Mary."

She tied the laces. "Oh, Mum."

"Oh, all right." She opened the front door. "Let's go."

Mary pulled the elastic from her hair and re-tied it.

Mary hated hospitals. The medical paraphernalia made her uneasy, with all the posted instructions and schemes for disposal of blood and syringes. People milling about in backwards housecoats drifted down the corridors, waiting for clean towels, food, or time to pass faster.

Just beyond a trolley spilling over with laundered linens and cotton thermal blankets was Intensive Care. Mary's mum slowed her pace and treaded more softly as she rounded the corner.

The first thing Mary saw was a man lying prone on a bed with a yellow sheet drawn up to his chin. In fact, it was really the nose she saw, with nostrils like two footprints side by side. Any movement and sound in the room came from the machines surrounding him—a heart monitor humming and an IV dripping a solution into the tubing that led to the man's arm. A light buzzed behind him. Mary wondered at his pitiable condition and watched with astonishment as her mother drew alongside the bed and put her hand on his forehead. "Hello, Dad," she whispered.

This pale, slight man was not Mary's Grandad! It was impossible! Grandad was tall and robust, pink cheeked and cheerful.

"It's Nora, Dad." Mary's mother took his hand in hers. "It's me and Mary."

Grandad's eyes fluttered open. He looked without expression first at his daughter and then at his granddaughter. His eyes closed again. Mary clutched her card tighter.

"Wait here," said Mum. "I'm going to speak with the nurse."

Mary stood silently, glancing around the room at the sea of warnings, tubing, and pumps. The place possessed a heartbeat all its own, a sort of droning up and down like a boat engine. She had the nerve to look at him again, at his white arms, his face with tiny veins on his cheeks, and the shocking shape of his skull beneath his skin.

"He's only just come out of his operation," said Mum, as she pulled a chair beside Grandad's bed. "He's on a lot of morphine for the pain."

Mary turned and found another chair. She dragged it across the floor and as she did so, the slight scraping of metal caused Grandad to wince as if the sound pained him, and then his eyes opened as before, but this time, there was recognition.

"Mary?" he said in a croaking whisper. "Dear Mary. Is it *really* you?" His eyes were wide with wonder as he stared at her.

Mary was surprised to be acknowledged before Mum, but felt she must immediately respond. She took a tentative step forward, clutching her get-well card. "How do you feel? I made this for you." She opened it up to the watercolor she'd painted on the inside. "It's my cat Doris, on the windowsill."

Grandad's eyes closed, and reopened as though he'd seen a ghost. "So good of you to come all this way. Been such a long time. You look just as you did when we were children. *Amazing.*" Then he reached his thin hand for Mary's, and grasped it as firmly as he could manage, straining to get his head off the pillow unsuccessfully. "I never meant any harm," he said, looking soulfully into her eyes. "I never wanted anything bad to happen to any of us. I suppose . . ." His eyes closed as he lost his train of thought and tried to retrieve it.

Mary looked nervously at Mum. "Why is he saying this stuff?"

Mum moved in closer to her father. "Dad, it's *Nora*, and I've brought Mary. My *daughter* Mary."

Grandad's eyebrows knit in confusion and without opening his eyes again, he spoke. "My leg is very painful. Call Dr. Cathcart."

"I'll get the nurse." Nora Devon rose to find the nurse while Mary sat still beside her grandfather.

His eyes remained closed as she found a spot on his bedside table for the card. Above his bed was a slip of paper in a plastic case that read *Humphrey Mills*. She looked down at him again and her eyes welled with tears. She swallowed hard, trying to choke them back in case he awoke again. Fixed on the rise and fall of his chest and the rhythmic beat on the monitor at his bedside, Mary didn't notice Mum and the nurse return to the room. Grandad opened his eyes as they entered and, seeing that he still possessed her hand, smiled adoringly at her and fell back asleep.

"Thanks for bringing in his things," said the nurse as she injected something into the IV drip and noted it on his chart. "I think it best that your grandfather rest now." The nurse winked at Mary. "He'll be more lively in the morning, don't worry." She pulled a thermometer from her pocket. Mary wasn't much comforted by the nurse's words. She almost wished she hadn't seen him so frail and muddled.

Mary was barely in the hallway before she started firing questions at her mother. "Why did Grandad say *I didn't mean any harm?*" she began.

Nora Devon adjusted her glasses. "I think it's as though he's dreaming," she said.

Mary ran her fingers through her bangs. "How could Grandad ever harm anyone?"

"Dreams are crazy," said Mum. "They don't always make sense."

"Well, I must really look like his sister when she was young or he wouldn't have grabbed my hand like that." They exited to the parking lot. "I mean, Grandad really thought that I was his sister Mary! Did you see his face light up when he saw me? Why would he be so thrilled to see her; hasn't he seen her for a long time or something?"

Mum sighed as she unlocked the car door. "Oh Mary, I don't know. He's confused. He's on morphine. He's been through a lot and he hasn't seen us for a while." She started the engine and Mary stared out the window. Mum reached across and held Mary's hand. "Let's just let it rest until tomorrow. I'm sure he'll be back to normal. You'll see."

Mary looked out into the darkness of the countryside. Only the fence posts and highway markers flashed in the car's headlights. But what kept flashing through Mary's mind was how desperately grateful Grandad was to take her hand in his, and how determined he was not to let it go.

Chapter Three

Mary felt as though she'd been awake for an eternity, and yet an unsettled feeling kept her from wanting to go to bed. Mum still buzzed about the house, likely operating on the same energy.

Mary wandered to the window, halfway down the hall toward Grandad's room. Here she paused, and looked out to sea. The window was open slightly and the salt air blew easily in.

Once in Grandad's room, Mary noticed a photo she hadn't seen before, on the wall by the chair. Herself and Kip, her brother, when they were small, perched on their parents' laps like balls of dough. But it was the collection of photographs on the dresser that enchanted her.

The photograph of Grandad's family was odd. Rudyard Mills, Mary's great grandfather, looked a good deal older than his wife, and much older than he was in the portrait on the landing. His face and beard were long, his hat and coat were dark, and it looked as though the sheer weight of them caused his shoulders to slope inward. Mary was drawn to the depths of his eyes, cheerless and dashed. His wife was looking sidelong at their children, inspecting appearance.

Mary felt suddenly light-headed and chilled. She snatched the photo from the dresser and sat down in Grandad's ancient armchair, stretching her legs straight. The chair was huge and welcomed her with down-filled cushions and well-worn upholstery. One of the arms was tattered and chewed as if it had been a puppy's object of attention for an unsupervised evening. Mary smoothed her hands over it, as she gazed into the faces of the Mills family. Then her eyes stung from tiredness and she rubbed them with her fists as a baby would. A wave of vulnerability washed over her like a draft.

Mary tugged a blanket off the bed. She draped it over herself and tucked the surplus between the cushion and the arms of the chair. While forcing the blanket deep into the crevices, Mary's fingertips found a hard object. She gripped it with her thumb and first finger, bringing it up into the light. A whistle, old and lint-covered. It was like the one Grandad used to call Jester, except the leather strap was dirty and worn.

Mary wrapped the whistle in the lower half of her T-shirt, polishing it gently as though she was cleaning a pair of glasses. She pulled it out and noticed the tiny scratches on its surface. The whistle warmed, producing a strange soft feeling.

Mary scanned the photo again. She could feel her great grandfather's worry, his sadness. Was his exhaustion now hers? There was Mary, Grandad's sister, looking all the while like Mary herself. An odd angle to her nose, yes, and the eyes were the same color and shape. Weird. It was definitely weird. The likeness was unmistakable. Mary felt a welling up of deep emotion, as though she was losing control, like when she caught a chill on the Ottawa River and couldn't stop her teeth chattering. She wrapped her fist around the whistle and squeezed, sponging up its warmth like water.

She felt compelled to put the whistle to her lips, blowing a single, sharp note.

Even as the tone of the whistle was still ringing in her ear, Mary's muscles twitched like they do sometimes when sleep is almost certain. Her eyes grew heavy. She struggled to open them, but felt a dizzying vortex drawing her down. Gripping the chair's arms couldn't stop her from whirling on and on through an enveloping space. Panic overwhelmed her, as she fought against a numbing feeling. It felt as if all her muscles and bones were draining away until the only feeling left was her heart lashing at her rib cage.

Though her eyes were squeezed tight to endure the sensation, Mary could make out an airy body in the blackness of her mind. She saw a ghostly shape in the distance that looked all the while like herself—spinning in synchrony with Mary, willing her toward it, closer and closer, until they were one. At this moment, Mary felt a welcome calm.

A breeze bathed her face. Leaves rustled. Mary stretched her toes and felt her calf muscles tighten.

"Mary!" came a distant voice.

She opened her eyes and found that she was lying in a grassy field with plump red hens chaotically pecking at the dirt and pulling at her long, black boot laces.

She gathered her skirts and stood straight in the sunlight, her hand shielding her eyes from the noon glare.

Humphrey ran toward her. "Did you put Miss Milk in the barn?"

"Ages ago," she grinned. "And do you know what?"

"What?" her brother asked.

"I have the feeling she'll have her calf today!" Mary grabbed the front of her skirts in a clump and started to run. "This'll be the day we get our first calf. I'm so excited! Let's race!"

A clean wind picked wisps of fair hair from Mary's braid as she raced Humphrey to the front porch. She whirled around and plunked herself down on the bottom step seconds after her brother tagged the porch railing.

"If I had longs like you," she puffed, "I'd win."

"That's no excuse. Anyway, I don't see why you can't wear longs," Humphrey said, as he sat down beside her. "Out of the question in England, I mean, but why can't girls wear longs in Canada?"

"Ask Mother." Mary smoothed her skirts over her knees, purposefully and with a question poised on her lips. "Why do you always win at races when we're so close in age?"

Humphrey strangled a grin. "You're fast for a girl."

"Am I?"

Humphrey nodded encouragingly. "There aren't a lot of fourteen-year-old girls who even run at all." Humphrey drew a stone from his pocket and threw it. "They think it isn't ladylike."

The front door opened.

"There you are." Mother smiled. "The soup will be stone cold if you don't hurry up."

Mary and Humphrey followed her into the house and closed the door. Mary slid onto a chair between Rachael and Eleanor.

"Where've you been?" asked Rachael. She knew the rules and, because she was six years old herself, broke them often. "The baby's getting angry and Mother gave her something before grace."

Mary leaned closer to baby Eleanor's high chair and stroked the sticky fist. "What have you got, Elly?" The baby grinned at her sister and Mary continued, "I think we're going to have our first calf today! I think Miss Milk is going to have a baby . . . just like you!"

Everyone laughed and little Eleanor joined in, slapping her plump palms on the wooden tabletop. Rachael looped her arm around Mary's. "Miss Milk's baby won't look like Eleanor," she said. "She'll look like Miss Milk."

"You're exactly right," said Mother, who bowed her head in quick prayer.

Mary slipped a small spoon into the baby's fist. "There, Elly, now you can have your soup."

The sun shone through the front windows and brightened their table.

"Where's Vera?" asked Mary, as she dipped a bread crust into her soup.

Mother's hair was washed in the light. "Still at Mr. Robinson's." She paused while she ran her spoon through her soup. "Miss Milk will need special attention, Mary. You and Rachael could keep her company until Father's home."

"And me?" asked Humphrey expectantly.

But Mary knew that her poor brother would have a stack of chores to do because he was the only boy in the family.

"Humphrey," said Mother, "you need to finish what you started this morning."

"Oh, Mummy," pleaded Mary like a bleating goat. "How often has Humphrey seen a calf being born? Can't he come with me?" She winked at her brother. "Please? I'll help him finish his chores later."

Mother dipped a cloth into a bowl of kettle water and wrung it out. "Wash your face, Elly," she said as she handed the warm cloth to her daughter. The baby sloppily smeared the cloth around her nose, then hung it over the edge of the table and watched it drop to the floor.

Mother scooped Eleanor from her high chair, planted her on her hip and said, "Let's all visit Miss Milk before we get on with our chores."

The five of them trotted down the porch steps and headed for the barn. Nell, the dog, rose from her basket and followed.

"Come ah, Nellie!" called Eleanor as she watched the brown dog follow.

"Come on, Nell!" yelled Rachael as she ran at top speed to the barn. Mary and Humphrey let Rachael win as she slammed into the barn door.

"Gently!" called Mother. "You'll startle her!"

The children slowed like stalking creatures, creeping over the straw toward Miss Milk. She mournfully mooed and reached round to scratch her side.

"Why don't you finish the wood, Humphrey, and I'll clean up the dishes with Eleanor." She put the baby down for a moment as she pulled a loose pin from her hair and reattached it. "Mary, you're in charge of Rachael, and Rachael, mind your sister."

Rachael nodded as though she intended to obey.

Mother smiled wryly. "And when you're finished, Humphrey, you may join your sisters if you like." She pulled her watch from her dress pocket and checked the time. "I thought Vera would be home by now. If she turns up, send her to the house."

Mary looked up at Mother, pink-cheeked and fresh. "I love having you with us, Mummy."

"It's certainly a change, isn't it?" Mother stroked the cow's broad face.

"We see you so much more in Canada." Mary fiddled with the straw at her fingertips. "I mean, I liked Miss Gough, but . . ."

"Miss Gough was wicked!" Humphrey interrupted. "I far prefer Miss Leigh."

"Miss Leigh is a nurse, darling," teased Mother. "She wasn't capable of schooling a naughty boy!"

Mary laughed. "Miss Leigh was heavenly. Eleanor loved her, too. We all did. But I mean since we *had* to come to Canada, at least we see more of you now. That's one good thing."

Mother smiled. "You're a dear girl to always look on the positive side of things." She watched Eleanor playing in the straw. "And I know it isn't always easy to do."

Rachael piped up. "I still don't understand why we moved here."

Humphrey and Mary glanced at each other, knowing that Rachael had broached a taboo subject. Mother stared down at her with an expression of conflicting emotions.

Chapter Four

Eleanor ran out the open barn door into the sunlight, and Mother was summoned into action. The baby lunged after the chickens at an unsteady gait, delighting in her ability to scatter them.

"Hey! Hey!" she shouted, blissfully unaware that at any moment she might fall flat on her face.

Eleanor broke into uncontrollable giggling as she toddled toward the front steps with Mother in pursuit. In a moment, they were inside the house, the door closed behind them.

The three older children were left in the barn. Humphrey seemed reluctant to exchange such a pleasant environment for one of drudgery. He sat on a bale beside Mary, while Rachael climbed up the stack, singing all the way.

"I was wondering what Mother would say—I mean, about why we came here," Mary started.

Humphrey nodded. "Me, too."

They were silent until Mary spoke as though she was thinking aloud. "Father started going on such long walks with the dogs."

Humphrey nodded but didn't look over.

"Even at night." Mary played with the end of her braid. "And he grew such a wicked temper."

Humphrey laughed.

"But he did!" Mary smiled. "Didn't he? Just about the time the men started to come and talk with him in the office."

Humphrey closed his eyes. "Yes, he did." He put his hands behind his head. "And then he called us all in to announce he was leaving the rectory."

"And Mother said he'd been there since 1900!"

Humphrey sighed. "Twelve years."

"At first I thought he was just leaving the rectory.' Mary remembered the shock. "I didn't think he meant we were leaving the country!"

Humphrey opened his eyes and fussed with his suspenders. "Exchanging Beddington for the wilderness of British Columbia!" He stood and ineffectively dusted himself off. "I'd better finish the wood before Father finds me in here."

Mary gave him a sympathetic look. "I'll help you when I can. It's just I'm supposed to stay here for the moment and watch Rachael . . . and Miss Milk, too." And then in response to Humphrey's look of resigned frustration, Mary added, "It's dreadfully unfair, all the chores Father has you doing because you're a boy. I wish I could chop wood. And stack it. I love that sort of thing!"

Humphrey looked cheered by her understanding. "Thanks."

Mary persuaded Rachael to come down slowly from the stack of straw bales where she stood like a goat on the side of a mountain. The sisters settled themselves and stretched their legs out straight. Rachael's blonde head rested gently on Mary's shoulder, and after a trying ten minutes of incessant questions regarding how a baby is born, Rachael fell asleep, her mouth gaping open like a cod's.

Mary had time to think about the previous conversation. She remembered that Vera had been exceedingly anxious about the disruption in Beddington. As the eldest child in the family, she was beginning to be treated as a young woman, and couldn't imagine herself on some hilly place picking peaches.

Despite the children's protestations, Miss Leigh and Miss Gough were dismissed. Auctioneers arrived to size up furniture and silverware, including a special set of silver trays with an engraved *M* in the center of each piece. Father seemed to spend all his time selling things off, with very little time at the rectory. When his tired and treasured Bible appeared one day on his desk at home, Mary knew for sure that he was leaving the rectory and more certain than ever that they would be leaving England.

Perhaps most upsetting for the children was finding homes for the animals. Dear old Grandmama adopted the two favorite tabby cats, Kathleen and Margaret. The others found homes with friends and neighbors. But there were unending tears over Nell, the most treasured of the dogs, and it was decided that they would attempt to bring her with them.

Mr. Hazel, the gardener, and dear Mrs. Wood, the cook, were regretfully dismissed with references when Father announced he'd purchased passage from Liverpool to Canada. Despite having shaken up all their lives without much discussion, he himself didn't appear to be overly cheerful about his decision.

He sailed alone, leaving his family to pack and await word. He spent a fortnight touring East Kootenay on horseback, finally finding twenty acres with a small house and two barns, one that could likely be converted to a church. By the time the rest of the family had reached Bircher by train coming from the east, Mr. Wilks, the north neighbor, had installed a cow as a welcoming present.

Mary heard the birds fly in and out of the barn, gathering straw and fur for their nests in the rafters, safe, up high, and unseen. She mused on this new life around her, Miss Milk's baby in the womb still, not knowing about grass and buttercups. The eggs developing in the mother birds, and the new green shoots and leaves unfurling each sunny day, more and more as if in the darkness of night the trees conspired to change the landscape from gray to green.

Mary heard footsteps, and through the door rushed Vera, flushed and warm, as she whirled down next to Mary. "I'm utterly exhausted!" she said as she put her flattened hand on her chest.

"All this time at Mr. Robinson's?" Mary asked as she stroked Rachael's hair. "Mother wants you in the house."

"The poor man can barely fend for himself." She leaned forward and crawled carefully to Miss Milk. "He had a woman who came twice a week to make a meal and do a wash, but she took a job with a notary." Vera stroked the cow's face. "Where's Father?"

"Mending fences."

Vera leaned back on the straw bale beside her sisters. Miss Milk began to moan low and deep. Mary and Vera watched the cow as she groaned and rested her chin on the bedding.

"Jenny Finch said it hurt her sister a lot to have a baby," said Vera, reattaching the pins in her hair. "She said that she screamed for ages. She said that she didn't scream like *eeee* when you see a ghost, but like *ahhh* in a growlish way."

"You missed lunch," answered Mary.

"I made soup for Mr. Robinson."

"You'd better go and help Mother," said Mary—reluctantly, since she was happy for Vera's company.

Father appeared in the doorway, Nell at his side.

He carefully stepped across the straw towards the cow. "Perhaps we'll have a calf by nightfall." He crouched low and stroked her neck. His hands were lined and fingers long.

"I'm going to fetch Wilks," he said as he unbuttoned his jacket. "I'm not entirely comfortable with this business."

Then he reached into his shirt pocket and pulled out a dog whistle attached to a braided leather strap. "Blow on this if you're at all worried." He placed it in Mary's hand, and, as if to emphasize its use, he used his other hand to close Mary's fingers around the whistle. Immediately, Mary felt warmth in the whistle, and softness as if it was malleable. For a fleeting moment, she felt light-headed, almost dizzy.

Rudyard Mills stood up and scooped the drooping Rachael into his arms. "Your mother likely needs help in the house, Vera," he said.

Mary was alone with Miss Milk and the chirping homemakers overhead. She thought to herself how lucky she was to be the third-born child. Vera, the oldest at sixteen, did most of the domestic duties with Mother. Humphrey, as the only son, had the lion's share of repair work and wood gathering. That allowed Mary some freedom unknown to the elder ones and as yet unwanted by the younger two. She tipped her head back onto the straw bale and watched the shadows in the rafters, the sun shining through the door and lighting up the air-borne dust and insects. She turned over names in her head. Alice, Emily, Barbara, Enid, Irene. Martha was her friend back in England. Surely she'd be honored to have a calf named for her.

Mary began to daydream. She thought about her best friend Martha, Miss Gough's grammar lessons, Kathleen sharpening her claws on the fence post, and then her old bedroom with pretty rose wallpaper. She remembered lying on the thick carpet in the dining room with the sun streaming in the windows, and how easy it was to fall asleep there, until Henderson came in to get the cutlery from the sideboard. As Mary remembered the watercress sandwiches, cakes, and thick cream laid out for the daily tea, she was jarred into her present reality by an enormous grunt from Miss Milk.

The cow pulled herself into a standing position and fluid spilled from her in a rush. Then the balloon sac burst and there were two hooves and the calf's face, the tongue sticking out. With another contraction, the big ears popped out, first one then the other. The new mother, calf, and Mary shared an identical expression of bewilderment and helplessness. Miss Milk lay back down on the straw, and, with one final push, the new calf entered the world looking as though it were encased in slug slime.

There followed a moment of utter and complete silence, as though Mary was witnessing the entire event on the other side of a window. Then panic set in.

Mary blew the whistle as loud as she could in the direction of the house. The shrillness was startling and a sudden dizziness forced her to close her eyes in an effort to keep it at bay. She felt warm and then burning hot. Veering out of control, her limbs tingled as though her circulation was returning from a bout of pins and needles, a mixture of pain, some relief and finally, confusion.

The phone was ringing. Her eyes flew open and she was sitting still in Grandad's bedroom, wholly exhausted, disbelieving that it would ever be possible to stand up, let alone walk. Her legs were like jelly and her back drenched in sweat. *What had happened? Why couldn't she move??* This must be a dream. And with that, she tried to stand and fell forward, taking the shock with her arms and shoulders, the strain of it making her feel vaguely ill. She rolled onto her side. The phone stopped ringing. She waited for what seemed a long time before it felt as though her body regained its former integrity.

Mum appeared at the door. "Why are you lying there like a dog? Did you get the phone? I heard it ring."

"No." Mary was shocked at her ability to speak. She sat up.

Mum drew the curtains. "I took the garbage out to the garage, and I heard the phone, but as I rushed to get to it, I stubbed my toe on that old steel bed. Serves me right for not putting my shoes on." She looked at Mary. "Are you okay?"

Mary shuddered. "I'm just really tired."

"It's been an exhausting day. Let's have a cup of tea and head to bed."

Mary nodded and slipped the whistle deep into her pocket.

Chapter Five

Mary sat in the living room feeling like Lucy having just returned from Narnia. She sipped her tea, puzzling over what had just happened to her.

"I've had the strangest dream," she said.

"When?" Mum sipped her tea and put her feet up on another chair.

"Just now."

Mum looked at her over the top of her glasses. "Now?"

"When I was in Grandad's room."

"You fell asleep in Grandad's room?"

"I think so." Mary slid down in her seat a little. "And I dreamt about Grandad's sister Mary." She studied her mother's face for a reaction. "And there were others."

"Is that why you were lying on the floor like a dog?"

Mary thought that Mum wasn't taking this very seriously. And why should she? It was just a dream, wasn't it?

Mary put her mug on a coaster. "It was sort of a nightmare, too. I mean, the whole thing sort of made me feel panicky and kind of sick."

"That can happen. One minute the dream is steaming along just fine, you're flying with birds or something, and the next moment you're being shot at, or plummeting out of control. I used to have flying dreams but I had to dodge hydro lines and people reaching up and trying to grab my feet. It was awful. But the flying part was wonderful!"

With that, Mary assembled her thoughts into a tidy package so that she could bundle the whole thing away and put her mind at rest. She was overtired, hadn't eaten well, and had been emotionally drained seeing Grandad so ill. End of story.

"Can we get Jester from the Kellys?" she proposed, feeling somewhat light-hearted.

"I don't want to be responsible for you spoiling him." Mum closed her eyes and rubbed them. "My poor grandmother had to pluck her husband's birds."

"If I was married to a guy who shot birds," said Mary, "I'd say 'pluck it yourself'." She tucked her feet underneath her bottom. "On second thought, I'd never marry a guy who shoots birds in the first place."

Mum smiled. "They were from a different generation. It wasn't the eighties. People are a lot more sensitive now."

Mary rolled her eyes.

"Grandad grew up hunting with his father. He didn't like it and told me once that he'd only shot two birds in his life. He couldn't stand to do it, to watch them fall from the sky. But his father made him help in any case. And so he grew up training his dogs as if they were hunting dogs. That's all he knew.

"When Grandad was a child in England, his father bought a piece of land in the Kootenays. He sent for his family and they came by boat to Montreal, then by train to Bircher." She turned the ring on her finger. "Your great grandfather was a rector, and he didn't know the first thing about farming. Suddenly he owns twenty acres of land with no well!"

"No water?"

"No water."

"What did they do?"

"They got drillers and his wife prayed a lot!"

"Did it work?"

"After a time, the driller found water."

They carried their mugs to the kitchen. "Why'd he buy so much crummy land?"

"That's just the way the land was sold. I suppose he didn't stop to think about whether there was a problem with the water."

"Then what?"

"He converted a barn on the property into a church, but he had very little money and he had to feed his family."

Goose bumps popped up on Mary's arms. "Did he have a cow?"

"A cow?"

Mary nodded.

"I don't know. I don't think so."

Mary felt the cold creeping through the window and drew her shoulders forward.

"We could use a fire tonight," said Mum. "Rain's in the forecast." She stretched her legs out straight under the table. "I stayed up past midnight getting your brother's things organized so Dad would know what was going on."

Mary yawned. "I'm so cold, my legs ache. And my stomach hurts."

"You've got travelitis—too much airplane air and not enough sleep. Go to bed."

Mary felt an overwhelming sense of contentment as she slid under the clean white sheets. She fell into a deep sleep within minutes, only to awaken three hours later in a panic.

"Mum!"

"Mary!" Mum gasped, as she leaped from her bed. "What's going on?"

"Someone's trying to break in!" Mary whispered, "Downstairs! Listen!"

They stood frozen together, listening to an unnerving scraping sound.

"Someone's trying to pick the lock!" Mary's voice jumped an octave. "Do something, Mum!"

Her mother raced down the hallway to Grandad's bedroom and reached for the phone. Mary followed. Then they heard a long, low howling.

"A wolf!" Mary gripped her mother's arm.

Mum put the phone down and flicked on the hall light. The scratching and howling grew louder. They approached the back door warily.

"It's trying to get inside!" shrieked Mary just before her mother switched on the kitchen light.

"There's your wolf," said Mum.

"Jester!" Mary opened the door and the black lab barrelled into the kitchen, his sopping tail wagging frantically as he weaved back and forth from Mary to her mother, joyous to be back in his home digs.

"I'll call the Kellys," said Mum, and she headed to the front hall table for the phone book.

Mary gave Jester fresh water and biscuits, and watched as he circulated through the downstairs rooms looking for Grandad. Mum kneeled down and dried the dog with an old towel. "Mrs. Kelly's so relieved. She said that they heard a whistle this evening and Jester went crazy. They took him out on a lead so he wouldn't run home, but by midnight he was whining up a storm, so she let him out to have a pee and he ran off." Jester licked her hand. "Mr. Kelly's coming over in the morning with his blanket and bowls." She watched her daughter cradling the dog's face in her arms. "Happy he's home?"

"Yeah," Mary cooed. "Look at his scroonchy-up face. He's got such nice loose skin!"

"It's two o'clock," said her mum. "Let's look at his nice loose skin in the morning."

"I'm too excited, Mum." She gazed down at the dog. "And so's he. I'll stay up with him just until he's settled down."

"It's cold down here, Mary, and you haven't got your slippers on."

Mary angled Jester's face toward her mum. "He says, 'I'm so happy to be home, but I need to cuddle with someone to calm me down.' " Mary gently held the tips of Jester's ears up to look like a dingo. " 'My, but you have lovely pajamas!' "

Mum laughed. "All right. Put him in his bedroom before you come up, and turn off the lights."

When Mum went upstairs, Jester ambled into Grandad's den, sidled over to the desk and lay down on an old square of carpeting underneath it. Mary turned on an old metal lamp, then slipped under the desk with the dog.

She patted his head, and, when he rested it between his paws, Mary noticed a painting behind him, leaning against the wall. It was partially concealed behind the back of the desk. All she could see was the face of a young child and someone's chin higher up.

"Come here, Jester," said Mary as she lured the dog away from his bed. Mary crawled back under the desk and carefully slid the picture out from underneath, and into the light of the lamp.

The portrait was an oil painting of a woman, slim and attractive with her hair neat and whirled behind her head. In her lap sat a baby with blonde curls, blue eyes, and plump arms, clutching a small, stuffed cat. Both were smiling. Mary had seen a portrait of her mum, and this little girl wasn't her. The baby's mother looked familiar, but Mary couldn't think from where. She slid the portrait back behind the desk.

The wind whipped the forsythia branches against the windowpanes. *Tap, tap, tap.* Mary's feet were cold, so she sleepily pulled a wool throw rug from the chesterfield and arranged it over her. *Woosh* went the wind as it whistled down the chimney and rattled the damper. Mary's eyes grew heavy. Her brain urged her to get up and go to bed, but her body ached.

She laid her head down and heard the sound of Jester lapping the water from his dish in the kitchen. She didn't feel right or well. Her ears were ringing and her head was heavy.

Slipping her hands into her pajama pockets to warm them, Mary discovered the whistle. She felt an immediate comfort from its familiar smoothness, as well as a strange urgency to blow it. Yet there was something inside her fighting against it, struggling with her emotions. Mary put the whistle to her lips and closed her eyes, succumbing to the dizzying panic. Swiftly and surely, she was embraced in a troubling descent. In the shadows of her consciousness was the other body, spinning in symphony with hers, until they were married into one. Mary's body relaxed into the union and accompanying peace.

Mary heard a rustling. She opened her eyes and the newborn calf struggled to right itself in the golden straw.

"Martha," whispered Mary. "We'll call her Martha."

"Martha it is!" said Mr. Wilks with a laugh.

Chapter Six

The children gathered in a mob, marveling.

Father stood in the doorway, holding tight to Nell's leather collar. "What now?"

"She'll be up within the hour," said Mr. Wilks. "The mother'll help her. Let me know if she doesn't." Then he straightened from a squat and walked outside the barn with Father. "I'll drop round in the morning and see how they're doing."

"Thank you, Angus," said Father. He started with Humphrey toward the house.

Mary barely noticed her father's leaving. She was enraptured by Martha and by Miss Milk. "She seems to know *exactly* how to be a mother."

"It's wonderful!" said Vera. "And now we've got two!"

"I want to call her Tree Trunk," said Rachael indignantly. "You name everything."

"I've only named Martha," returned Mary. "Mrs. Wilks named Miss Milk."

"*Anyway*," hammered Rachael, "I didn't name no one."

"*Any* one," said Mary. "I'd just very much like to name her after Martha Mitchell Banks." She marveled at the calf. "As a sort of way of remembering her." They all turned to the calf and watched as the brown fur began to dry and soften.

"Tree Trunk?" said Vera. "What are you on about anyway, Rachael?"

Rachael folded her slender arms. "She's the color of a tree trunk, and her fur's all swirly, like bark."

Mary smiled at Rachael. "Maybe that could be her middle name: Martha Tree Trunk Mills."

Rachael clapped her hands together. "Father can baptize her!"

"He'd *never* do that," said Vera.

"We could do it in secret," Mary whispered. "When Father's not about."

They giggled and nodded in agreement. Mary wondered whether Rachael was old enough to keep a secret, even one as absurd as this.

The next morning, Mary awoke as the sun slid through a crack in the curtains. This day was so bright and wondrous that Mary would remember it long after they'd left Bircher.

She chose not to risk waking the others by dressing, so she wrapped a blanket around her shoulders and went silently down the narrow staircase and into the kitchen. Nell looked up at her and wagged. Mary grinned and smoothed her hand over Nell's sleek brown head and ears. She glanced in the direction of her parents' bedroom.

Mary slid on her boots and tied the laces while Nell worked playfully at trying to lick her face. Quietly unbolting the door, Mary slipped into the shiny new day with the dog bounding before her.

She raced across the wet grass to the barn, Nell at her side. When they reached the barn door, she looked down at the dog. "Wait here."

Mary was startled to find Humphrey, sitting in the straw.

"Good morning!" he said, cheerily.

She scooted beside him, delighted to have company. "What are you doing here?"

"Same as you," said Humphrey. "Spending time with our new baby!"

The small barn had a radiance all its own as shafts of light squeezed through the cracks and shone on the calf and mother. The barn smelled of love—joy and awe and the magnificence of life.

Mary stood and approached the calf slowly. "Morning, Martha," she whispered.

Miss Milk looked at Mary. Mary grinned, and reached out to the calf. The mother struggled to her feet and Martha followed suit, shakily standing, steadying herself into nursing position. Miss Milk seemed to enjoy Mary gently stroking her face from her forehead down to her moist, whiskery nose. She was tranquil.

After a time, Mary sat down with Humphrey and covered them both with the blanket. Neither spoke much, content to watch the calf sleep and the birds build their nests. Mary hadn't any idea how long they'd been in the barn, when Father appeared in the doorway.

"How is our new calf?" he asked.

"She's *so* amazing, Father. Such a miracle."

Humphrey lazily got to his feet.

"You can't go to church wrapped in a blanket," Father said, looking down at his daughter. "Back to the house and into your clothes, both of you. I'm off now to prepare." He disappeared out the door.

Humphrey and Mary reluctantly headed into the sunlight. It was transformed now, from the soft white light of dawn to the constant warmth of morning. Mary believed that dawn was made for the animals. It was their time of day to be alone and peaceful, not yet mindful of the human animals who housed, hunted, or trapped them. Preparatory time. A gathering of strength. She could feel a sense of it herself. She understood the early morning, whether dull, or brilliant like this morning, to be essential.

Rachael appeared out the front door in a clean dress and washed boots. Then Vera appeared with Eleanor on her hip.

"You'd better hurry up," said Vera. "Mother's dressing and it's almost time for the service." She watched as Mary slid her boots off. "Were you going to attend in a nightshirt?"

Humphrey slipped past her to change and Mary didn't answer. She took the stairs in twos, pulled off her nightshirt, and slipped into a blue, paisley print dress. She tugged a comb through her long hair. Mary didn't care for dressing up. She wished she could wear longs every day as Humphrey did.

Mother was standing in front of the mirror, persuading strands of hair to stay where she put them. "Ready?" she asked, distractedly.

"I'll braid my hair as we walk." Mary pulled the length of her hair into three equal parts. She stood by the door waiting for someone to open it so she wouldn't have to let go of the braid she'd started.

Mother smoothed imagined creases from her own dress, first in the front, then in the back. It was a green, floral print dress with a cream collar and a good length of pretty buttons. Mary thought she looked beautiful. Her wispy, brown hair had the slightest suggestion of orange, like autumn leaves as they start to turn, and her eyes were the color of her dress. She was slim, yet Mary realized for the first time how strong and capable her mother was.

In England, she was the mother who received and sent invitations to parties and dances. She organized meals, the children's clothes, vases of fresh flowers on the piano, and schooling. In Canada, Mother performed entirely new duties in the confines of this small home. She did the washing, cooking, scrubbing of floors, changing Eleanor's soakers, preserving food. She fed the chickens, gathered eggs, picked berries.

Mother's job also extended to her husband's position as rector, to see to it that the people of Bircher saw in the Mills family a fortitude they could rely on. If Father was to be the clergyman of choice, then he must be seen as having a tight and harmonious family himself. And Mother must be seen not only as the capable mother and wife she was, but as the church secretary, social directress, and diplomat she would have to become. If Reverend Mills was to be revered, his family would have to be admired.

She and Mary hustled out the door. They walked along the dirt trail leading up the hill to the church. Mary could see a few people standing outside and wondered how many were already inside.

"Don't rush," said Mother quietly. "Walk steadily, all together." She put one vertical finger to her lips and looked severe.

The family filed into the church. Vera passed Eleanor to her mother and they formed a neat row along the first of six pews. Mary noticed three or four other families and she could hear more coming in behind them.

When Father appeared, he was obviously pleased at the turnout. His sermon was all about helping each other in times of need. This, as everyone knew, referred to the Clement family whose horse had fallen from the steep cliff on their farm into the river and had washed up on the beach some days later. And as the horse was an integral part of the threshing machine, John Clement needed some help with his farm, and perhaps in the acquisition of a new horse.

A few of the children leaned into each other and whispered about the decomposing horse and how it smelled like skunk. Father interrupted the muffled giggling by announcing an unplanned hymn, "Oh God, Our Help in Ages Past." Mary wanted to sing today, swaying with Eleanor when it was her turn to try and curtail the baby's boredom.

Coming out into the sunshine, Mary felt a sense of relief, for not having to be inside anymore, for not having to sit on the hard pew and for the rare look of happiness on her father's face. This was only his third sermon, and it seemed that each one attracted at least one newcomer. This time it was a Mrs. Sutherland, a widow and well-known pianist.

Mother chatted easily with the women about the latest fabric at the Bircher Mercantile Company, about the recent arrival of Dr. Cathcart who had left a successful medical practice in London to emigrate with his wife and three young sons, and about Phillip and Irene McDewey who had left for the coast to work at the general store in Port Haney.

The children raced around playing tag. Mary stood behind her father, slightly at a distance, wanting to congratulate him on the service, to encourage his congeniality. When she saw an opportunity and approached closer, a man she'd never seen before eased forward and leaned toward her father.

"Robinson's a loner, you know," he muttered. "Not a church-going fellow."

"Oh?" said Mary's father.

The man continued awkwardly. "You may want to keep an eye on your daughter, the one who helps with the housework."

"Yes," said Mary's father, distractedly. "Yes, thank you. Thank you indeed."

"The new fences look grand," said the man, as if trying to balance the seriousness of his last comment.

Reverend Mills looked around him at the new fences he and Humphrey had erected. "Rather," he said with a terse smile. "Thank you."

The man tipped his hat to Mary's father and turned away.

It was Mary's turn to speak softly. "It was a wonderful sermon, Father," she whispered. "Look at all the people!"

Reverend Mills put a hand on his daughter's shoulder and smiled. "The family looked first rate in the front pew, what?" He looked toward the children who were running circles around baby Eleanor. "Mind your sister."

When most of the town's families had dispersed, the Mills family headed for home. Humphrey, Mary, and Rachael raced down the grassy slope until they reached the shade of the front porch.

"Nell!" called Rachael. "Come on, Nell!"

They sat on the front steps, waiting for their parents. As Father approached, he pulled the dog whistle from his pocket, put it to his lips and blew a sharp rolling note.

The children watched the woods, until Nell sprang through the trees with a limp rabbit in her mouth. Rachael screamed and Mary lost her balance fleetingly, shut her eyes tight, closing up this world in an involuntary start. She felt a swelling of emotion, a searing heat, and then an extreme heaviness in her arms and legs. A cool hand soothed her burning forehead and her eyes fluttered open.

"You've got a fever, dear," said Mum. "Sit up and drink this."

Chapter Seven

Mary sipped the flat ginger ale, immediate relief for her lips and throat.

"You'll feel better in your own bed," said Mum. "Let's get you upstairs."

A soft bed was a great relief. Mum opened the window just enough for the air to circulate. She straightened the bedding and tucked in the sides, snug but not tight. On the bedside table, she put the glass of flat ginger ale, a thermometer, and some medication.

"Take these." She handed two tablets to Mary.

Mary chewed the tablets and lowered her head onto the pillow. "I had another dream," she whispered. "About Grandad's family."

"How nice." Mum slid into her bed. She turned out the light and settled herself onto the pillow.

Mary was too tired and ill to pursue the myriad feelings swarming about her head. Her dreams seemed so *real*. They were like nothing she'd ever experienced. The details were vivid and sequential. Peculiarly, the dreams drained her energy and rendered her weakened for a short time. Perhaps it was simply the onset of fever.

Mary spent two more days inside the four walls, her fever advancing and retreating. Both mornings, Mum went to the hospital to see Grandad. During this time, Mrs. Kelly came into the house as a precaution, though she made it quite clear that she was fearful of germs and so never actually entered the guest room. Instead, she called from the bottom of the staircase, "Anything you need, dear?"

The inquiry inevitably jarred Mary awake, so that she wanted to yell down, "A little peace and quiet." But instead, she said, "No, thank you," as politely as possible.

"You've picked this up on the plane," Mrs. Kelly said after her umpteenth wake-up call. "Or the boat. Everyone gets sick on planes and boats."

Mary never actually laid eyes on the woman, and so conjured up a very unflattering image of her. It would have been more complimentary had she not been so irritating.

By the third day, Mary felt well enough to sit up in bed and draw in her sketchbook. But once she'd sketched the chair, the dresser, the window, and wastebasket, she took to reading instead. It was decided that she was well enough to be left alone when Mum went to the hospital.

One evening, on just such an occasion, Mary went down to Grandad's den and pulled the portrait from behind the desk. She propped it against the chesterfield, then stepped back and stared. The tapering light of dusk shone through the den windows and gave Mary a new perspective of the subjects.

The mother was beautiful. Her hair, like so many Mills people, was substantial yet wispy. Tied and wound into a bun at the back, the neatly brushed brown hair framed her face perfectly. Her neck was graceful and long above a neat dress collar. Her eyes were olive, her lips pink. The woman was serene, perhaps reflecting the contentment she felt with the child in her lap.

The child looked like a girl, with loose blonde curls that fell short of her small shoulders. She wore a white smock, no shoes or socks, and held a little stuffed cat sewn with tidy blanket stitches.

Mary left the portrait on the chesterfield, and went to the kitchen. As she was recovering, so was her appetite. She made a grilled cheese sandwich in the old iron frying pan, and while it was browning on the stove, she set a place for herself in the dining room.

"Now," she said to Jester, who followed her from the kitchen to the dining room, hoping for a handout, "we'll need a spoon for the peaches and a glass for juice and a little nibbly for you, Mr. Whiskerino."

Mary slid her hot sandwich on a plate and sat down. Jester lay beside her, shifting his nose back and forth in expectant hope of careless manners.

"Enjoy," she said to Jester, lowering the toasted bread crusts into his grateful mouth.

Mary heard her mother's car and went to open the front door.

"Well, don't you look recovered!" said her mum.

"I feel recovered," said Mary. "Can I visit Grandad tomorrow?"

Mum slid off her shoes. "Yes," she said. "He's got another day of physiotherapy and then he'll be coming home."

"How long are we staying?" asked Mary.

"We'll leave when Aunt Hester arrives."

Mary rinsed her dishes under the tap. "From Tofino?"

Her mother put the kettle on. "She doesn't come down to the city much, if at all; hates it, in fact."

"But this isn't the city."

"It is compared to Tofino," said Mum. She took a tea bag from a tin.

"Why's she coming?"

"For Grandad." She rinsed the teapot with hot water. "I phoned his sisters in England who are all quite busy with their own lives. Then I phoned Aunt Mary, and Hester volunteered to come and take care of him for the summer. I didn't even ask—she just suggested it would be a good idea for her to come." Mum put some cookies on a plate, and then on the tray.

"Does Aunt Hester have kids?"

"No." She poured milk into the mugs. "She never married, and she's too old for that sort of thing now. Into her late sixties, if I'm not mistaken."

"Why can't *we* take care of him?"

"We have to get back home." She filled the teapot with boiling water. "I've tried to persuade Grandad to come to Ottawa with us, but he won't. To be fair, it's a long way to travel and far too hot in the summer."

Mary loved the short drive from Grandad's home to the hospital. The countryside was spectacularly green from spring rains. Daffodils and grape hyacinth congregated amidst tall grass at the roadside, warmed now by the sun's touch.

She was giddy to find Grandad looking so well. He was propped up in bed reading *The Economist*, and she had mere seconds to observe him before he peeked over his bifocals and said, "Well, well, well, who have we here?"

"Me, silly," said Mary as she ran to him with a hug that was sure and loving. "You look so much better, Grandad."

He was pale and lean, but his eyes danced as he patted the bed beside him. "Now what is all this about stomach flu?" he asked. "And who gave you permission to grow?"

Mary looked sheepishly at Mum and pointed. "She did."

They laughed and Mum mockingly complained that Mary frequently borrowed her best sweaters.

Just then, Grandad's lunch arrived, so early in the day it seemed, and presented in a mustard-colored, inelegant plastic mold.

He surveyed the tray and grimaced. "Dreadful," he muttered. "They've given me ear wax soup."

"Cauliflower," said Mum, as she leaned over and looked at the menu request form. "Didn't you ask for this?"

"I asked for chocolate cake." Grandad winked at Mary and tentatively guided his spoon through the soup. "I don't think this could be any less appealing."

Mum adjusted her glasses. "Why don't I bring you something you like?"

He smiled appreciatively and then turned his attention to Mary. "You look so like my sister when she was a girl." He looked amazed, somewhat wistful. "The same hair, blue eyes, and shape of face, even." He put down his spoon and dabbed at his mouth and mustache with the paper napkin. "She was slight—like you, Mary—but tough as nails. Very much a tomboy, always wanting to wear longs."

"That's my Mary," Mum nodded. "I cannot get her into a dress to save my life."

Mary laughed. "Why would anyone want to wear a dress? You can't run in a dress or stand on your head . . ."

"Well, you can," Mum interrupted.

"But it's not very ladylike," finished Grandad.

Suddenly there was a blip in Mary's mind, as if she was watching TV and unexpectedly a second of another show flashed on screen and then was gone. *Mary, wearing a dress, sitting on a porch beside a boy.* And that was all. It was over and closing her eyes couldn't bring the image back.

"The sight of you will make me well in no time," said Grandad. He reluctantly picked at his lunch.

Mary told Grandad all about Jester stealing home in the night, about Mrs. Kelly coming in when she was sick, and how she sat up in bed and sketched every piece of furniture in the guest room.

A nurse appeared and suggested Grandad rest before his physiotherapy session. He was clearly downcast. "She has spoken," he declared.

"Aunt Hester comes soon," said Mum. "It'll be so good to see her again."

"Grandad," Mary ventured, as she zipped up her sweater, "who are the people in the portrait behind your desk?"

The very second Mary uttered the word "portrait," Grandad's face fell. He looked stung and Mary regretted mentioning it at all. Before Grandad could find words, Mary's mum whisked the book from his bedside table and asked what he was reading. A short discussion followed and then Mary was first to make amends and hug him.

Grandad's mood picked up. "They'll be coming to torture me soon," he smiled. "Want to stay and watch?"

"Behave," said Mum.

"Why did Grandad look so sad when I asked about the portrait?"

Mary's mother focused on the highway curving in front of them. "It's weird and I don't know the whole story, but I do know that you'd better not ask any more questions."

"Why?"

"When I was a kid, I found that portrait hanging in his closet, behind his clothes. I thought it was the strangest thing that he'd hang a painting where it couldn't be seen . . . at least by most people."

"And?"

"I asked him about it and he went silent just like he did today."

"Why?"

"You keep asking me that and what I'm trying to tell you is that it's a secret. Even my mother refused to talk about it, which wasn't a surprise, as there were a lot of things she wouldn't discuss."

"Did you see the portrait in the den?" asked Mary.

"I didn't know it was in the den now."

Mary glanced out at the green fields along the highway. "I found it behind his desk, the night I got the flu."

"You'd better not ask him about it again." Mum pulled the car into the driveway and Mary noticed at once that the gate had been left open.

"Oh, Mum!" she shrieked. "Jester's out!"

Mary raced through the gate and along the path beside the house. She called his name as she ran down the dirt trail to the beach. Panting and calling still louder, she raced back up to the lawn and waited for the sound of his jangling dog tags. Nothing.

Could he have returned to the Kellys' in confusion? Or did he take off in search of Grandad? Mary slid a hand into her jeans pocket and felt the whistle. She clutched it and in so doing, felt drawn to it as before, to call the dog home, but for what other reason? Why was she blowing into this thing as if it could save her life? There *was* something else, *she felt it.*

A familiar fatigue overcame her and she sat on the grass. She must be tired from the visit to the hospital, still taxed from the flu. No, it *wasn't* that. It was something else that weakened her to the core and flooded her with crazy emotion. She panicked, struggling to fight it, yet wanting to let it grip her. Mary lay back and waited. The vertigo, numbness, down and down with only her heart boldly beating the few seconds before she'd reach the ghostly figure, the other body that seemed all the while a part of her soul. A peaceful lull followed, interrupted by Rachael's mournful tears.

"It's all right," said Mary soothingly. "It's Nell's instinct to kill rabbits. She's not a bad dog." Mary wiped a tear from Rachael's face. "The rabbit wouldn't have suffered. She would've died with very little pain."

"It's still dead," Rachael sobbed. "It's dead, dead, dead!"

Chapter Eight

"There, there," said Mary as she rocked her sister back and forth.

"We'll eat it," said Father.

"How revolting," said Mary, wrinkling up her nose. "I'm not eating the poor little thing."

"You'll eat what you're given." Father seized Nell's collar, and retrieved the limp rabbit from her mouth. "Out!" he commanded. Then he looked hard at his daughters. "You ate plenty of rabbit in England. You just didn't see it before it lay on your plate."

The children watched as Father walked to the house and disappeared inside. The door closed.

"I'm going to visit Martha Tree Trunk!" said Rachael as she dramatically whirled off toward the barn. "Martha! Oh, Martha! Here comes sister Rachael!"

"Our little Rachael's joining the nunnery!" winked Humphrey.

Mary laughed and sat on the steps. "Father will be pleased!" Then her face fell again. "I don't understand why Father's become so bad-tempered and wicked."

Humphrey sat beside her and they lay back on the front porch, letting the sun soak into their formal clothes. It wasn't long before Mother appeared, calling them in for soup.

The children were chatty about the successful service.

"It was the best ever!" said Humphrey. "They rather liked the topic, I think."

Father cleared his throat. "I trust it'll be of some benefit."

Mary liked the singing in church. That was it. She hated to dress up, hated to sit still, hated trying to keep Eleanor quiet. Mostly, she hated the frustration of trying to remember how to behave just so, to feel the weight of expectation on her.

She was thankful that one of Father's parishioners had given Mother a handful of fresh dill that made an immense difference to the flavour of today's soup.

After lunch, Mary and her siblings dispersed into the yawning afternoon. Eleanor, who had almost fallen asleep in her soup, was freshly pinned and bundled up in a wool blanket. She slept like a hibernating creature on Mother and Father's bed.

Rachael and Mary had disappeared to the barn, where they sprawled out on the straw near Miss Milk and Martha Tree Trunk. Humphrey went behind the barn to split wood. Vera was off to Mr. Robinson's, as usual. Mother baked bread.

At dinner, Vera felt sick. She couldn't eat the rabbit and this upset Father. Mary ate around the rabbit, refusing to even taste it, fretting all the while about what she would say if Father noticed. Eleanor took the meat morsels in stride, ignorant of their origins. Rachael ate uneasily, her eyes cast down. Humphrey ate out of duty. All in all, it was a frightful meal.

When the dishes were washed and put away, the children gathered on the floor in front of Father while he read from the Bible. Vera, her face pale and uneasy, asked to be excused so she might lie down. Rachael claimed to also suffer from stomach upset, but looked fairly full of beans. Father told her that she must stay and listen but she could stretch out on the carpet with her head in Mary's lap. Father wasn't one for excuses.

Soon, the light in the house grew dim. Father lit the kerosene lamps so the children could wash their faces, hands, and feet before crawling into their beds. He abandoned the nighttime ritual to Mother as usual, pulled on his overcoat, and headed for the door.

"I've paperwork to complete," he mumbled as he called Nell to heel.

Mary watched Mother pull the curtain aside and she, too, could see the lantern light bounce about in the darkness like a garden fairy. It faded as Father ascended the hill to his little church, then there was no light, and Mother let the curtain fall closed.

Rachael had quickly fallen asleep—as a method for avoiding the vile-tasting tooth powder—when Mary slipped under the blankets beside Vera.

"Good night," said Mother from the bottom of the stairs.

"Good night, Mother," Mary whispered back.

"Night, Mother," said Vera.

As Mary settled into bed, she listened to the soothing sounds of Mother tidying the kitchen and preparing for tomorrow. Then Mother's bedroom door creaked closed and the house itself seemed to relax its joists and floorboards, grumbling as the warm air slipped through the cracks between the logs. All was still except for Vera's whisper.

"Mary?"

"Yes?"

"I think . . . I mean, I'm sure . . ."

"What?"

"I have the most dreadful, um . . ." Vera's voice broke.

"Whatever's the matter?"

Now Vera sobbed.

"*Do* talk to me, dear Vera! What *is* it?"

Vera pulled a handkerchief from her sleeve and quietly blew her nose. She sat upright. "I'm . . ."

"You're *what*, for God's sake!?"

Vera whispered, "I'm with child."

Mary felt her face grow cold. "You're not!"

"I am."

"But you *can't* be, it's not possible!"

Vera pulled a cushion from the bed and sobbed into it. Mary put an arm around her sister.

"There, there," Mary soothed. "I'm sure you're mistaken."

"I'm sure I'm not."

"*How* can you be sure?"

"Oh Mary, it's no use denying it. I wouldn't have told you had I not been absolutely sure."

Mary looked into her sister's blotchy face.

"I don't know what to do," whispered Vera after a moment. "What should I do, Mary? I don't know what to do!"

Mary squeezed her hand. "Let me think."

Mary felt panicked. Her head raced. *With child!* How strange it sounded to even *think* the word in her head. What could be worse? What could be worse for Father, for his parish, for the Mills family? What could be worse in the whole world? In this moment of awareness and desperate understanding, Mary wished they were still in England, back in the old house with the cats, the comforts. This couldn't have happened in Beddington, not in their little village, not to Vera, not to *any*one.

England was a place of nurses and governesses and green gardens and dear Grandmama. Roasts on Sunday, people in to tea with so many tasty cakes, croquet on the lawn by the drive. Not one single person that Mary knew in England was ever with child who wasn't supposed to be with child. It just didn't happen.

Mary turned again to Vera and whispered in her ear, "Who is the father?"

"James, of course," said Vera.

Mary gasped. "He's a *grown man!*"

"Oh *Mary* . . . of *course* he's a man."

"And he's obviously taken advantage of the situation."

"That's just it, Mary, he hasn't entirely, I . . . ."

"You *what?*"

"I love him very, *very* much, and he's longing to marry me."

Mary was startled. James Robinson wanting to marry Vera was preposterous enough. The fact that she was already carrying his baby was the very pinnacle of the unimaginable.

Vera worked the blanket edge with her fingers. "Father would *never* allow it. He'll have my head when he finds out."

The worst possible thought that Mary could think of was the prospect of Father finding out. Mother was a close second. And for a fleeting moment, Mary thought of Grandmama finding out, and how horrified she'd be that Vera, all of sixteen, was with child out of wedlock. Mary imagined the old woman, mouth gaping, falling backwards in a faint.

Vera rolled onto her side, her head resting on her bent arm. Mary assumed the same position and they stared at each other.

Mary took Vera's hand in hers and searched her sister's olive eyes. "Oh, Vera." Mary caught a tear streaking Vera's cheek.

"James was an orphan, you know," whispered Vera. "He grew up in an orphanage and left when he was fifteen. That's why he's so reclusive, I think. That's why he paints and lives off in the woods."

Vera's voice faltered as she turned and sobbed into the pillow. Mary rubbed her back around and around, circling, like the thoughts in her head.

"Don't cry, Vera," she said soothingly, like Mother would. "We'll think of something. We'll think of something." But Mary was really thinking that if Vera kept crying and Mother heard, what excuse would she give?

"I love him," blurted Vera. "I love that he's so kind and gentle and quiet." She turned and cried again into the soaked pillow. "I think that he could be happy. What will Father do? He'll murder me, Mary! He'll absolutely murder me!" She pulled a fresh handkerchief from her dress pocket draped over the bedside chair. "Don't you remember that awful Ronald Talbot who Father said would end up at Oxford, and wouldn't he just be a striking fellow and intelligent, and wasn't it a good idea to have him 'round so I could meet him? Don't you remember how he had that positively *revolting* breath and he was blathering on and on about how good he was at lawn tennis and cricket, and oh— I couldn't wait to see him out of the house! Don't you remember *dreadful* Ronald Talbot?"

Mary nodded, "I do remember. He was a beastly poser."

"Well, that's the man Father had his eye on for me. That's the type. I heard him telling Mother one day. I overheard them speaking about it. He said that in the not so distant future we'd make a smashing couple, he being Lord Talbot's only son and all that rot. He was planning on becoming a surgeon, do you remember? And that impressed Father a lot."

"I *do* remember Father going on and on about him one morning, and I even remember that very evening while I was bathing, I thought up a verse about him, and it was about Ronnie being scrawny."

Vera stared incredulously at her sister. "You say the oddest things sometimes." She paused. "You'd like James. He has an interesting mind like yours. He's always thinking, even though he's quiet. He's so very intelligent but he hasn't the need to let everyone know it. He sometimes reminds me of Mr. Bainsbridge back home. And you know, he's an artist like you. A really good one. He paints like we read." She dabbed at her eyes again and then fell into sobbing.

"Vera, it's all right. Everything will be all right."

"He's going to murder me."

Mary took Vera's hand again. The room was growing cool now and Rachael in her sleep tugged the blankets up to her chin and coiled into a ball, blissfully unaware of the drama unfolding beside her.

"He won't murder you."

"He will. And what's worse is that he's been ever so strange since coming to Canada. He seems forever lost in thought— worried about us, I suspect. I suppose that's what makes him so foul tempered. So how do I help things along? This! This is how I help things along." Her voice broke again. "It's a nightmare, it truly is . . . when I wake in the morning, I scarcely believe it's all happening. Before I open my eyes, I *will* myself to be home in England. And then I open my eyes and see these wooden walls, so primitive and bare."

Mary was thinking along the same lines. This was a nightmare. She rolled onto her back, still holding her sister's hand. "We're both worn out. We can't lie awake all night fretting over it." Mary pulled a strand of hair from Vera's face as she so often did with Rachael. "Let's sleep now and we'll talk more in the morning." And then with a heavy heart, Mary fell asleep.

Chapter Nine

When Mary awoke early the next morning, she was confused by the quiet in the house. Vera was gone, and Rachael lay sleeping, her mouth open wide, her arms flung out from her body as if she'd been picked up and dropped like a rag doll.

Mary crept down the stairs, but there was no Nell to lick her feet as usual. The door was not bolted, so Mary went directly outside into the crisp morning air and ran to the barn. There she found Vera draped over a bucket, throwing up.

"Oh, *dear* Vera!" said Mary, as she went immediately to her sister's side and put a hand on her curved back. "What is Father going to think when he sees you?"

And even before Mary saw Vera's expression of horror and desperation, she regretted those words.

"I feel so *sick*," sobbed Vera. "I can't hide this any longer." She put her hand over her belly. "I know I don't *look* very big, but I can barely get my skirts buttoned!"

Mary stared at her sister's mid-section. "When is the baby due?"

Vera lifted her head from the pail. "December."

"Christmas?"

"Christmas." Vera let out a great moan and retched over the bucket again.

Mary heard Nell barking and had mere seconds to think of a plan. She whipped the bucket from under Vera's head and put it behind a straw bale. The cow and Vera had the same quizzical look at the moment Reverend Mills strode into the barn.

He sniffed the air, the unmistakable scent of vomit. Mary was certain he'd ask about it.

"Breakfast!" he said with the same drama with which he said, "God!" in church. Then he headed back to the house.

Vera put her hands on her hips as she straightened up. "Good gracious, how am I ever going to get through breakfast?"

"Tell them you've eaten. Carry on normally. Go to Mr. Robinson's house as usual."

Vera dusted off her skirts. She took pins from her pockets and pulled her hair back with them. She had a momentary calm about her, maybe because she'd been crying.

She stood in the sunlight streaming through the barn door. She was mother's physical double, thought Mary, though Vera didn't have the strength of an army the way mother did. And now, Mary worried, what little strength Vera had would wither away with the worry of it all.

Vera bundled up a few things in the house and quickly left.

"Bye-bye Veewa!" called Eleanor as Vera waved to her seated siblings at the door.

"She looks pale," said Mother after Vera closed the door.

"She woke up early," said Mary. "We're not used to the heat upstairs." Mary popped a potato chunk into Eleanor's mouth.

Mother poured boiling water from the kettle into her cup. "If it gets too hot, you'll simply have to put your bedding downstairs."

"Doesn't she have chores to do here first?" asked Reverend Mills.

Mother took her plate to the sink. "Mr. Robinson gives a fair wage, and he's got work in the morning for her. She can do her chores before tea."

Father looked down in thought.

Over breakfast, Rachael talked of Miss Milk and Martha, while Humphrey and Mary discussed Mrs. Daly's apple tree that had come down in a wind. Then Father went up the hill to the church and they all got on with the business of the morning.

Many more days passed in the usual way. Then one morning, mother needed eggs for a lemon cake. She was halfway to the barn before Mary heard the screen door slam. By the time Mary reached the barn, Mother was immobile, staring at her oldest daughter doubled over and throwing up.

Vera's head remained level with the bucket, her eyes fixed on Mother. Mother gave a horrified gasp and put her hand on her chest. It seemed as if she'd never exhale.

She ran to Vera and put her hands on her daughter's shoulders, shaking them in fury and frustration. Mary tried to pry Mother's fingers from her sister's shoulders, but the two were caught in an odd paralysis, staring into one another's eyes.

Mother finally put her hands on her hips. "It's Mr.Robinson, isn't it?"

Vera looked down. "Yes."

"Good *God*, what are we to do? How *could* he have done this to you? We trusted him. Mr. Wilks even said . . ."

"Said what?"

"Said he was not God-fearing."

Vera let go her mother's hands and wrapped her arms around herself. "Just because he doesn't believe in God, it doesn't make him bad," she implored. "In fact, he's a damn sight more kind than most of the people in Father's bloody church!"

"Vera!" Mother pulled back her shoulders and put a hand over her mouth.

"Is Mr. Wilks the one who decides who is good and kind around here?" Tears streamed down Vera's face. "Is he God? *No!* He's a *gossip!*"

There followed a silence permeated with astonishment and dread. Vera flung herself into Mary's arms where she cried her soul out. It took a moment before Mother had fully digested Vera's uncharacteristic outburst. Then she, too, wrapped her arms around Vera and cried.

Vera drew a handkerchief from her pocket and blew her nose. "James is a *very* kind man, Mother. I *love* him and he loves me and isn't that important?" She swallowed hard and spoke in a tiny voice. "Oh, what shall I do?"

Mother wrapped her arms around Vera and Vera hugged Mother in return. They stood for a long time, leaning against each other, tears sliding over their cheeks, down their necks, to be eventually absorbed by the material of their dresses.

Everyone's desperation was thick in the air, and the fact that Mother was desperate at all so bothered Mary that she plunged into the embrace a second time. And this act alone was like a trigger that shot Mother back into the driving seat. She straightened her spine, pulled her shoulders back, and wiped the tears from her face with the knuckle of her index finger.

"Come," she said.

Mother sat down on the straw and drew the girls with her.

When they were settled, Mother asked, "You're certain it's Mr. Robinson?"

"Mother!"

"My darling, I'm sorry." She paused. "Will he marry you?"

Vera visibly perked up, suspecting Mother had a feasible plan. "He's longing to."

"I know this sounds a strange question," said Mother carefully, "but is he as peculiar as everyone says he is?"

Vera looked pained. "Not in the least, Mother." She fiddled with the grass. "As I told you, he's very kind and sensitive. It's just that he's ever so quiet and he's nervous of people and he's . . ."

"What?" She stroked her daughter's hair.

"He was orphaned at four years old, when his parents drowned in the lake. He lived in the orphanage until he was old enough to earn a wage, then apprenticed with a milliner for a time before learning farm work. He likes being outdoors because it gives him ideas for his paintings. And I think . . ." she twirled her hair in thought, "that the other reason he likes working outdoors is that working inside—in an office, I mean—maybe makes him feel as though he's confined, as he was at the orphanage. Sort of trapped. And I think he likes being alone in the woods because he was with all the other children growing up—for every meal, school, holidays, bedtime." She paused, but only briefly, as there seemed to be much to say in his defense. "It can't have been easy, living in there all those years with never any nice mother or father coming to take him away to a home of his own."

Mother looked blank, and Mary wasn't sure whether the most problematic aspect for her was the fact that Mr. Robinson was an orphan, or that there wasn't much in the way of lineage.

Mother put her hand on Vera's. "Father will have to know. He'll find out soon enough, and it's better that he's told, rather than figuring it out for himself."

Vera choked up again.

Mary squeezed closer to her sister.

"Let me tell him," said Mother. "If I don't do it now, I'll lose my resolve. I'll go now to the church. He'll be calmer in there. If we put it off, it'll fester in all of us."

"He'll murder me."

"He won't murder you, dear. Whatever happens, you're his firstborn child."

They walked hand in hand to the house where Rachael appeared, wiping the sleep from her eyes.

"I'm going to the church for a time, dear," said Mother. "You stay here with your sisters and tend to Eleanor when she wakes."

Mother disappeared up the hill and soon Humphrey showed up. He sat on the step and stared at his sisters, oblivious to the unfolding drama.

"You look dreadful," he said to Vera.

Mary glowered at Humphrey. She looked back to Vera sitting slumped on the step, looking shrunken in stature as her lips moved in silent prayer.

"It's going to pour," said Humphrey.

Mary went into the house and returned with Eleanor on her hip. The chickens strutted close to the front steps, pecking at the earth. Thunder boomed and it began to rain. The chickens turned tail and made for the barn.

"Goody!" shrieked Rachael, as she pulled up her nightdress and danced on the ground by the porch steps.

Then Eleanor struggled to be let down and raced around with Rachael under the shower.

Mary allowed herself to smile, because it was heart-warming to watch the little girls dance gleefully, so unknowing that they spun and twirled in the eye of a storm.

Mary noticed Vera's lips had grown pale. Father was striding toward the house.

Chapter Ten

Mary moved toward Vera and stood alongside her. The little girls slapped their filthy feet on the muddy earth as their sheer cotton nightdresses stuck to their legs. Humphrey stood still, as he so often did when his father approached.

"Come with me," Father commanded Vera, who reached for Mary's hand. Father glared at Mary. "*Alone.*" Rain flattened the old man's thinning hair to his head.

Vera reluctantly let Mary go, then turned and followed her father to the barn. Mother gathered the little ones inside. Mary sat on the porch steps, straining to listen. Humphrey sat beside her.

"What's all this about?" Humphrey whispered. "Father's *enraged.*"

There was no easy way to say it. "Vera is with child."

The corners of Humphrey's lips turned down and his eyes bugged out. "With child?"

Mary nodded.

"It's not possible."

She looked hard at her brother. "It is."

"Good *God*."

The shower eased to a mist and the steam began to rise from the soaked earth. After a time, Mary couldn't stand it anymore and walked cautiously to the barn. Humphrey stood. Before Mary reached the barn door, it flew open and Father strode out, scattering the chickens like birdseed.

Father put the whistle to his lips and blew long and loud. "Nell!" he croaked, as if he'd exhausted his vocal chords yelling at Vera.

Mary felt a shock, as if she'd put a stray hand on the stove by mistake. She knelt down, suspecting she might faint, and closed her eyes on this world. Warmth soothed her, snaking through muscles and bones, limbs and skin, until there was feeling again, a sensation that she had ownership of her body. She lay for what seemed a long time with her eyes closed, soaking up a sense of relief and return. A gentle tingling of tags snatched her attention.

"Jester!" She wrapped her arms around the dog's neck. Jester sniffed wildly, nuzzling her hand as if she held raw fish in her fists. Mum stood watching on the stair.

"There's something going on here," said Mary.

"One of us must have left the gate open, that's all." Mum adjusted her glasses.

Mary shielded her eyes from the sun. "No, I mean I had another weird dream."

"Another one?"

"Just now." Mary stroked Jester's head.

"You've been with me just now, dear." She turned to go back up the steps. "I think you're just remembering your dream from last night. Sort of a *déjà vu* kind of thing." Mum stuffed her hands into her back pockets. "I could use a hand tidying up."

In the front hall, Mum picked up the pile of clean, folded clothes at the bottom of the stairs and carried them up to the guest bedroom. Mary followed, still feeling unsteady. She fell backwards on her bed while Mum slid the clothes into drawers, then lay down on her own bed.

"I'm tired. Let's get the butler to tidy the house," said Mum.

"Okay," agreed Mary. "*Jester!*"

Jester bounded upstairs and onto the bed.

"Grandad will have a fit if he sees Jester in this state of indulgence." Mum put her hands behind her head.

Mary looked at her sidelong. "I don't think he would."

"You don't know him like I do." Mum polished her glasses on her T-shirt.

"Yes, I do."

Nora Devon smiled at her daughter's reply. "Hester's coming in the morning."

"That's great!" Mary sat up and crossed her legs. "He's finally coming home!"

"After his morning physio. Probably around eleven."

"Wow! I'm so glad!"

"Me, too." Mum sat up. "I hate seeing him in the hospital." She smoothed the quilt with her fingers. "I can't wait until he's home, in his own bed."

"Where's Aunt Hester going to sleep?" asked Mary.

Mum got up and straightened the blankets. "I should put her in here with me, really."

"Oh, come on, Mum, where am I going to go?"

"The den?"

"Put Aunt Hester in the den."

"Mary."

"Mum."

"Actually, the sensible thing would be for me to sleep on a cot in Grandad's room in case he needs me in the night," said Mum. "You and Hester can sleep in here."

Aunt Hester's bus arrived at the terminal in the morning.

"There she is," said Mum quietly, as though she needed to examine her before approaching.

Mary had a brief moment to check her out before greeting her, to notice that she was small, wore jeans and a sweater, and carried a blue backpack over her shoulders. Mary thought she looked younger than someone in her late sixties. She had a merriness about her.

"Aunt Hester!" Mum waved.

She smiled warmly. Compact and tidy, she looked as though she'd escaped from a Beatrix Potter book—Ginger came to mind, from *The Tale of Ginger and Pickles*—a neat and casually turned out yellow cat.

Hester gave Mum a substantial hug before moving on to Mary. A hugger, Mary thought, is usually a good sign.

"You must be Mary!" she said.

"I must be," said Mary, surprising herself, and then, "I mean, I am, yes . . . how do you do?"

Hester simply stared, grinning. "My, my. Look at you. Just *look* at you!"

Mum locked arms with Hester and the three of them walked into the shocking sunlight.

At home, they had tea together in the living room, where Mum pulled a third chair to the little round table by the window.

Here, they caught up on who was where and whose children had done what and, of course, Grandad's health.

Mostly Mary watched the women and let her mind wander, hurriedly finishing her own tiny cup of tea and her allotted take of the biscuits. Scanning the bay with the binoculars, Mary focused on a blue heron standing stock still on the rock, waiting for movement in the water. She grew impatient as the morning slipped into afternoon with nothing to show for it but a cold teapot and warm chairs.

Mary had long ago abandoned them and lay nearby on the dining room floor with her watercolors, painting the tulips and forget-me-nots with the sparkling sea beyond.

"Good grief!" Mum leaped to her feet. "I've got to get Dad!"

Aunt Hester followed Mum into the kitchen with the tea tray.

"Coming, Mary?" said Mum as she slipped on her sandals. "Unwind, Aunt Hester. Unpack while I'm gone. You must be exhausted from your journey." She searched for her keys in several pockets. "You and Mary are sharing the guest room. Put your things in the top two drawers. Make yourself at home."

Mum and Mary rushed out the door, into the car and off. Mary wondered how Aunt Hester could possibly unwind anymore. Wasn't she utterly unwound? In any case, they were off to the hospital now and all this unsettling part of the trip would be over. Grandad was coming home.

"Thanks for letting me stay in the guest room," said Mary. "I love the bed."

"It works out," said Mum.

The highway cut through lush fields dotted with sheep and lambs. The ewes grazed while their young ambled about. The day was bright, unfurling leaves even brighter beside the mature, dark green foliage. Fir trees sprouted pale tips. Dandelions lined the highway, the sun's loyal representatives, waving their cheerful round heads. It was surely spring and every living thing seemed to celebrate the warmth and strength of the sun. This day, Mary thought, was the perfect day to welcome Grandad home.

Grandad was sitting on the edge of his bed with his small suitcase beside him. His leg was in a cast with a thick, gray work sock stretched over the foot. On the other side of him was a pair of crutches, leaning against the bed.

"It's about time," he grinned.

"Sorry, Dad," said Mum, giving her father a peck on the cheek. "Aunt Hester arrived this morning and it's been a bit crazy."

"Take away the *C R* and substitute an *L*," added Mary.

Grandad smiled. "I'll be nursed by a pair of lounging lazy bums, will I?"

"You will," said Mary. "Aunt Hester drinks as much tea as Mum, and that'll leave about two hours in the day for taking care of you."

Mum frowned at Mary. "Shall we bring Grandad up to speed on Jester's recent adventures?"

Mary blushed.

"Shake a paw," said Mum as she offered a hand to her father. "Let's go home." She helped stabilize the crutches beneath his armpits.

Mary felt comfort seeing Grandad dressed in his own clothes—shirt, V neck sweater, and tweed sport jacket. He sat in the front seat of the car, drinking in the scenery. Mary could almost feel his relief at seeing his own house at the end of the driveway.

Aunt Hester stood in the doorway, eyes dancing with anticipation. "Uncle Humphrey!" she called, as he emerged from the car, "Uncle Humphrey!"

They hugged as if they might never let go; then Aunt Hester took Grandad's suitcase and kept pace with him as he hobbled toward the house.

"I've been inside for too long," said Grandad. "Could we sit in the sun for a time?"

"Good idea," said Mum. "I'll get a pillow."

"You sit with your grandfather for a minute, Mary. I'll be right along." Aunt Hester trotted after Mary's mum.

Mary and Grandad made their way along the brick path to the bench in the back yard. Mary was surprised how much he leaned on her while he lowered himself to sit. Jester peeled out the back door and whirled about at Grandad's feet, unable to contain his joy.

"Who have we here?" he laughed as the dog put his paws on Grandad's lap, straining to reach his face.

Grandad grinned with such affection that Mary was able to understand, in this moment of coming together, how utterly devoted to each other were the dog and the man. They respected each other, relied on each other, and loved each other. *A life is a life*, thought Mary. A beating heart is a beating heart, no matter the body in which it beats.

"I've taken care of him for you," Mary beamed.

"Well done," said Grandad as he sat and gently stroked Jester's head. "Well done."

Mum, Mary, Grandad, and Aunt Hester sat on the bench like birds on a wire, staring out to sea. Mary slipped her hand into her pocket and felt the whistle and leather strap. She found comfort in it. A power associated with it made her anxious and excited all at once. If she ever lost it, she felt as though she'd lose a part of herself.

Chapter Eleven

At breakfast the next morning, Mum announced that she and Mary would be leaving the following day.

"What? Are you crazy?" said Mary. "Grandad just got home!"

"I've talked it over with Grandad," said Mum, looking across the table at her father, "and we've decided that now that Aunt Hester's here, we should be getting home to Dad and Kip, and getting on with things there."

"What am I going to get on with, exactly?" asked Mary.

Her mother tapped her hard-boiled egg with a silver spoon and started to peel away the shell. "Summer, tennis lessons, painting classes, and all that fun stuff."

"Why can't we stay longer? Why can't we go home next week? We just *got* here!"

"I know it feels that way, but Dad's had to juggle his work schedule so that we could be here. We can't expect him to do everything forever." Mum filled Grandad's glass with grapefruit juice.

Mary sagged. "May I be excused?"

She ran down the trail to the beach, sat on a low log and scooped up a handful of stones. Mary let fall the round ones, sifted out the flat ones, then sent them skipping over the water. She didn't want to leave this place. She didn't want to go back to Ottawa now, to the sameness of life there. Tennis lessons, art classes, walking Mrs. Chin's dog every other day as she did every summer. Round and round the block on the sun-baked sidewalk. Sleeping in the dreadful heat with her fan whirring all night. Here she had the ocean breezes billowing the curtains. For the first time in a long time, she could sleep with pajamas and blankets. Mary felt a place for herself in this house, not just as a visitor or as a child to be cared for, but as a thread in the fabric of the family.

After a time, Mum appeared with a comforting arm around Mary's back. "I'm sorry I sort of sprung that on you, dear. I hadn't realized how much you were enjoying it here . . . spending these quiet days with me. I just thought you'd be missing all the kerfuffle at home."

"Why?"

"You did last time." Mum scooped up a handful of stones. "You couldn't wait to get home."

"That was different." She raked her hands through the rocks. "I was little."

Mum picked a pretty stone from her bunch and gave it to Mary. "Would you like to stay here with Grandad and Aunt Hester when I go back home?"

"Stay?"

"Stay."

Mary gave Mum a hug. "Oh thank you, thank you, thank you, thank you, thank you! For how long?"

"Grandad wants you for the summer, but I think maybe one or two weeks would be sufficient."

"The summer? The whole summer?"

"Aunt Hester says you'd be a big help taking care of Grandad and Jester . . ." Mum leaned closer in a conspiratorial gesture, " . . . not the way you've *been* taking care of Jester, mind you. And Grandad says he's barely seen you and would be willing to adopt you if we decide to give you up."

They laughed and Mum reached for Mary's hand. "Let's go inside and you and Hester and I can have a powwow about Grandad. He's resting on the couch."

The house was cool. They tiptoed past Grandad who lay snoring with his leg supported on a pillow, the paper open and flat on his chest. As they passed, he opened one eye and winked at Mary. She winked back and gave him a thumbs up. In the kitchen, Aunt Hester was washing the last of the breakfast dishes.

"Okay, nurses," said Mum, "Let's brief or de-brief or wear briefs or whatever."

It was decided that Mary would stay on for another two weeks with Aunt Hester and Grandad.

"Dad misses us all, and he's really going to miss you," said Mum. She paused. "I haven't left yet and I miss you already."

"Come on, Mum. Stiff upper lip and all that."

Aunt Hester took Mum's hand in hers. "She'll be fine, Nora. Go and pack."

Mary and Aunt Hester stood and watched as Mum walked through the turnstile and disappeared down the escalator. Mary felt a little like crying and a little like changing her mind, but not enough to do either. So she stood beside Aunt Hester, waving and watching until she could see her no more. They turned and Aunt Hester hooked Mary's arm into the crook of her own arm and lead her back to the car.

The day passed strangely for Mary, suddenly on her own, without the comfort of Mum. Mary, Grandad, and Aunt Hester formed their own family unit, three generations under one roof, although to Mary, it seemed simply as young (herself) and old (Grandad and Aunt Hester).

Mary was surprised that she found genuine companionship with these old people—nappers and bridge players. Sometime shufflers. Tea totalers. Mary was drawn to their easy rhythms, to their considerate natures, their honesty. Both liked to paint, as Mary did, and often they'd sit outside, or at the beach with brushes and watercolor block, recording the day with Alzarin Crimson, Cerulean Blue, Gamboge, Raw Sienna, and Sap Green. Courteously sharing brushes, discussing favorites, how to draw sea and sky, trees and birds.

After dinner, while Aunt Hester saw to Grandad's bath, Mary took Jester for a walk. They started on the winding road, with Jester on a lead. But Mary soon found the trail that took them through the woods. Jester strained on the lead, his nose to the ground where he caught the scent of deer, rabbits, and raccoons. Mary's arm ached and the pulling had no effect on Jester's thick neck. She unsnapped the clip so Jester could get some proper exercise, then off he went with his tail going side to side and his nose working much the same way.

Arching blackberry vines sprung across the path as Mary made her way along, carefully pulling the thick ones aside. She called Jester to make sure he was within earshot and he raced down the trail and almost knocked her over, smiling and panting, waiting for praise at his return. Then off he went again after some unseen prey. This went on for half an hour until the forest began to darken and Mary turned back. By now, Jester had chased numerous scents and trailed Mary with a happy tiredness.

Mary left Jester, flaked out and panting, on the kitchen linoleum. Bed was calling.

Aunt Hester was already in her pajamas, folding her clothes and putting them away in the drawers. Mary's eye caught a small, double frame with two photographs resting on the dresser. She studied it. To her surprise, one of the photographs was of the very same likeness as the portrait in Grandad's den. The other was of a different woman wearing pants and a sweater, her arm around a young child of about six who was holding tight to the collar of a dog. "I've seen a painting of that photograph on the left," said Mary tentatively, fearful that speaking of it would arouse the same mysterious response.

"My father painted that portrait. He was an artist." She moved beside Mary to look at the photo again. "When your Grandad was a young man, my father gave it to him."

Aunt Hester had never been stern before, but she gave Mary a severe look now. "Don't ask him about the portrait just now." She put the photo frame on the bedside table. "It upsets him. I want to focus our energy and his on healing his leg."

Brooding on Hester's reaction, Mary readied herself for bed.

"Good night, dear," said Aunt Hester.

"Good night."

Then Mary noticed a pile of change on the table, coins Aunt Hester had earlier taken from her jeans pocket. An arrowhead stood out in the pile, smooth and black.

"Aunt Hester?" she whispered.

"Yes, dear?"

"Where'd you get the arrowhead?"

"From your Grandad. It's my good luck charm." She pulled the covers under her chin and rolled onto her side. "It's been a long day."

Mary leaned over to the chair beside her bed and pulled the whistle from her shorts pocket. She put it on the table beside the arrowhead. "This is mine," she whispered.

Hester smiled. "Lovely."

"It's a whistle."

Her eyes were closed now. "Very nice."

"I found it."

Aunt Hester didn't answer. Mary thought her like a dog as she curled up and fell asleep, twitching and breathing deeply as her dreams unfolded. Mary stared at the ceiling. Her body felt tired, though her mind was racing—one minute to Ottawa, the next to her school, and then to this place where she now felt very much at home. She turned on her side and stared at the photographs on the table, the arrowhead, smooth and worn, and the whistle beside it.

Mary reached for the whistle. She wrapped it in her hand like a skipping stone, wishing on its strength. Goose bumps ran along her arms as her eyes fixed on the photograph, on the woman with the infant. She was family, somewhere in the fabric, and hadn't Mary met her recently? But how was that possible? Mary stared deep into her eyes, at her skin, her hair, her dress. *Vera. That's Vera.* Mary had the odd sensation of a dream making sense in the real world. There was a connection, she was sure of it.

Mary opened her hand. The whistle was warm now. It was silly to blow into such a thing in the night, with her old aunt curled up like a black bear. Yet she was compelled, and it seemed monumental to resist, like a cough that can't be suppressed. Yet the moment it reached her lips, she felt as though her lungs were drained of air. Loss of control meshed into a dizzying spell, and she knew as she plummeted that she'd been this way before and that she should relent and allow herself to slip around the inner edges of this whirling mass. Mary knew the worst was yet to come—the panic, loss of sensation, and a heartbeat gone mad. But this time, she longed to be with the other body, to reach it and meld with it as fast as she could. So immediate was the union that Mary was startled when her breath became suddenly gentle and her mind clear.

Chapter Twelve

Father's steps were so vigorous and angry that Mary veered out of his way and averted her eyes. She didn't look behind her, but slipped into the barn to find Vera slumped on the floor.

Mary wrapped her arms around her sister. "There, there, don't cry, it's all right."

"It's *not* all right," Vera moaned.

"What did he say?"

"Horrid things."

"What things?"

"Dreadful things."

"How dreadful?"

"Oh, Mary! He said I'm to go to Uncle Thomas and Aunt Barbara's house in Victoria until the baby's born and then I'm coming home and I'm forbidden to ever see James again!"

"But it's his baby, too!"

"He said I'm to give the baby up." Vera could barely speak. "He said no one's to know of this."

"When do you leave?"

"A week." Vera stared with bewilderment. "He's going to wire Aunt Barbara."

Mary gripped Vera's hand. "You *can't* go!"

"He said I had no business staying in the family in this condition." She broke into agonized tears. "He said I'd probably ruined his chances here, that I'd ruined everything for everyone, that I'd done a dreadful thing. That James is a bad sort—an artist—and not our kind." Vera blew her nose. "I've never felt so *wretched* in all my life." She paused for a moment, straightened her back, and spoke in a steadier voice. "I have to give the baby up. That's all there is to it."

"Do you want to give the baby up?"

Mother appeared and went straight to Vera. "Darling Vera, don't lose heart. Aunt Barbara and Uncle Angus are really rather nice and I'm sure . . ."

"I don't even *know* them!"

Mother held her hand. "You're feeling dreadful, and Father hasn't helped, but I think his plan is a good one."

"Giving away the baby is beastly," interrupted Mary. "Why can't she go away and have the baby and bring it home?"

"To Bircher? Father won't have it." Mother cleared her throat. "It'd be rather awkward, wouldn't it? The rector's own daughter with child. Can you imagine?"

"It's not Father's baby," said Mary.

Mother looked at Mary sternly. "Vera isn't married, Father doesn't believe Mr. Robinson to be a suitable husband, and this is not how one goes about beginning a family."

Father stormed out the door after dinner and returned a half an hour later. Dusk loomed. Eleanor was sound asleep. Humphrey lay on his bed. Rachael was singing quietly to herself upstairs in bed. Vera and Mary lay stock still beside her. They could hear Father mumbling to himself, then he was out the door again, and all was still until the first explosive *whack* of splitting wood. He worked for hours chopping and stacking, chopping and stacking in the light of an oil lamp.

Mary and Vera lay awake—reviewing all that had transpired.

"I'm almost seventeen," said Vera. "It could be worse. Nettie McComb can't be more than eighteen, and she's expecting her second child."

Mary was beyond tired but knew that her sister was rationalizing the circumstances. "I don't think it's your age that's got Father so agitated. I think it's more to do with James Robinson and the fact that you're not married." She sneezed. "Bless me. Nettie McComb's husband is a constable. No one really knows much about Mr. Robinson. He's rather a mystery."

"Not to me."

The house was peaceful and warm, and Mary anchored in her mind the belief that things would work out somehow.

In England, she remembered Miss Gough cutting short strips of ribbon and laying them on the fence rails for birds to find. Then later, when the fledglings had hatched and flown away, they'd spot a nest in a leafless tree and climb to claim the treasured nursery decorated in the finest silk ribbons and softest cat fur.

"What are you thinking?" whispered Vera.

Mary turned on her side toward Vera. "I was remembering Miss Gough and how she'd leave ribbon on the fence rails for the birds. Those fat mother birds worked endlessly getting their nests ready with little twigs and grass and things. It's really quite touching."

"Humphrey told me wolves mate for life," said Vera. "A male and female will remain together their entire lives."

"Like people." Mary pulled the bedcovers up to her chin.

"I suppose."

Vera twirled a strand of hair with her finger. "I wish we were more like animals. I wish all these social graces weren't so important. Don't you?"

In the morning, Nell set to howling when she heard footsteps on the stair outside. Father was up and washing. Mother was washing dishes. Eleanor started to cry, so Humphrey opened the door and greeted James Robinson, tall, lanky, and bearded.

"I've come to see your father," he said cautiously.

Father came alongside Humphrey. "What business have you here?"

"I've come to ask for permission to marry Vera," he said.

Vera stood with Mary at the top of the stairs.

Mother scooped Eleanor in her arms and watched the men slip outside and close the door behind them.

Mary and Vera hurried to the little loft window where they only just had room to peer out and see the tops of the two men's heads in front of the porch steps. Vera put her arm around her sister's waist.

Then James Robinson strode away, and the girls' heard the front door open and their father's recognizable footsteps.

There was a silence, as there is in all families as the frustration rises without any outlet, simmering at this unexpected turn of events, waiting for the pot lid to rattle and for the water to leak out onto the flame and burn, acrid and unwelcome. Even little Eleanor silently busied herself with a set of twigs she'd been collecting, lining them up on the floor like prone soldiers.

Mary slid on an old dress and Vera struggled with the largest one she could find, leaving several buttons undone and hiding this fact with an apron. Mother pulled bread from the oven and laid it on the table. Father stood staring as if he didn't know what to do next. But when Vera came down the stairs and stood in front of him, the seething frustration leaped into words and scorched her.

"I won't let you make me a laughing stock!" he bellowed. "You've sinned in the worst way, but I *won't* let him have you. You're better than he is." Father stuffed his pipe with tobacco. "You'll have the baby in Victoria and then you'll come home. Life will carry on and no one will be the wiser, and this emigration to Canada will not have been a *complete* waste of time."

Vera grit her teeth and looked a picture of fury.

"You *won't* see him again," said Father. "Is that absolutely clear?"

But before anyone could answer, he turned and disappeared out the door, Nell at his heel.

Mother, Humphrey, and Mary raced to the window and watched Father march up the hill to the church.

Even the dog didn't dare disobey him at this moment.

Chapter Thirteen

Since James had visited the house, Mary and Vera were trying their best to avoid Father. They'd uncharacteristically volunteered to clean the barn and were working hard to prolong the task. As Mary poured feed into the trough, the barn door burst open.

"I've a message for you!" panted Humphrey, as he strode toward Vera. "A note from Mr. Robinson!"

Mary's mouth fell open.

"Give it to me! Oh, when did you see him? What did he say?"

"I saw him at the general store," said Humphrey, breathing hard still. "He asked me to talk with him, then we went to his house where he wrote this note, and he wanted me to give it to you immediately."

Vera unfolded the letter with rising excitement and held it in a shaft of light streaming in between two uneven planks on the barn wall. The three of them clustered around the letter.

"What does he say?" Mary stood on her toes with excitement.

Vera beamed from ear to ear. "He says that he was asking Father's permission to marry me, but since he's not giving it, he wants to marry me anyway as long as I'll have him! It'll be against

Father's wishes, but he says it's best for everyone, and that he really loves me and . . . how dreadfully sorry he is and that . . ." She paused and looked first at Humphrey and then at Mary. "He's written a letter of apology to *Father*." Vera blushed. "The rest is rather personal." Vera folded the letter and held it tight.

"Heavens! That's grand!" said Humphrey, smiling.

"You needn't go to the coast, with any luck," clapped Mary.

"Yes, I know." Vera bit her lower lip. "But with the promise of a proper ceremony in Father's own church, and an apology on top of it all . . . he'll just have to agree. And I shan't be discouraged if he doesn't."

The three of them locked arms and hurried to the house. Bursting through the front door, they were surprised to find the south neighbor, Mrs. Saymer, seated at the table.

Mother seemed tense. "You remember Mrs. Saymer?"

"Yes," piped Rachael, "we just met."

"Yup," copied Eleanor.

"Yes." Vera extended her hand to the old woman. "How do you do."

"How do you do," echoed Humphrey, quietly retreating back out the door.

Mary reached out her hand and smiled.

Vera obviously didn't feel she could leave, so she sat beside Mary on the bench seat.

"I must be off," said Mrs. Saymer in an oily voice, before downing the tepid dregs of her teacup. "Lovely to see you."

"And you," said Mother. "Do come again." And that was the final bit of insincerity spoken before Mrs. Saymer lifted herself from the chair and mumbled, "Rather."

Mother watched out the window as Mrs. Saymer labored up the dirt path towards the church and road.

Mother turned to her daughters. "She knows."

Vera sighed. "I know."

"You knew that she knew?" asked Mary.

"Oh, stop it!" shouted Vera. "It's not funny."

"I'm not trying to be funny," said Mary.

"That's quite enough," said Mother. She smoothed her hair back. "Mrs. Saymer came to confirm her suspicions and now that her suspicions are confirmed without any details from me, she's off on her merry way."

Humphrey, having watched Mrs. Saymer leave, returned to the house. "Have you told Mother?" he asked.

"James desperately wants to marry me, Mother! He's agreed to a ceremony in the church and he's written Father an apology. Surely Father can't object to that."

Mother looked stunned. "But the arrangements . . ."

"We'll plan it!" said Vera.

"No, no, I mean the arrangements to stay with Aunt Barbara and Uncle Angus," said Mother.

"We'll cancel them," said Vera.

"Easily," said Mary.

"Rather," said Humphrey.

"Rather," said Rachael.

Eleanor twirled herself up in the bed clothes.

It was past midnight and Mary could hear her parents talking downstairs.

"I despise James Robinson," said Father. "He's taken advantage of Vera and offered marriage as a knee-jerk reaction to the pregnancy."

Mary could hear Mother trying to keep his voice down.

"He's a social misfit," he continued. "Self-absorbed." He paused. "But what's done is done. Vera is with child and that won't change."

"She loves James," said Mother. "I think he's right and honorable to ask for her hand in marriage." Mother's voice became quieter. "To be truthful, I'd be worried sick if Vera was staying with your brother in Victoria."

For a time, Mary heard nothing and wondered whether they'd fallen asleep. Then just as she turned on her side, Father began again.

"The wedding must be simple," he said. "With only family in attendance."

Mary elbowed Vera, who blinked her eyes and lifted her head. "What is it?"

"Shh!" whispered Mary. "They're talking about the wedding!"

Vera sat up. "What?"

"Shh!" Mary looked toward the door. "Mother and Father are discussing the wedding! *Your* wedding! Oh, Vera—Father will allow it!"

The girls hugged for a moment before Vera broke away with a smile from ear to ear. "Oh, Mary! I can't believe it!"

They strained their ears to listen, but the conversation was so hushed that gleaning any more information was impossible. They were content with the pleasing scraps they'd got, and both girls fell into a delicious slumber.

Mother set a date and Father planned a simple service. The day came with little fanfare and much anxiety.

Despite the somber glow cast by Father, there was some excitement and levity in the house after he disappeared up the hill to the church. Mary felt slightly giddy as she watched Mother take out her floral print green dress with the cream collar and pretty buttons. She smoothed the fabric, running her long fingers over the finery. Then from a wooden trunk under the bed, she took a smaller box and gave it to Vera.

Mother, Mary, Humphrey, and Rachael huddled around Vera as she slid the little latch aside and opened the hinged box to reveal two beautiful tortoiseshell combs.

Rachael drew in more than her share of air and put her hands on her face.

Humphrey and Mary drank in the astonishment on Vera's face.

"They were Grandmama's," said Mother. "I'd like you to have them now . . . and the dress." Mother put her capable hands on Vera's shoulders. They looked in each other's eyes, so similar in intensity. "Your grandfather did not approve of Father, you know," she said.

Mary raised her eyebrows. "Really?"

Mother looked at the girls in turn. "He wasn't financially secure and didn't show promise of being so. He's older than I by a fair bit, and that bothered my parents. But love is love and people have to find their own way and make do with the consequences. You will, too." Mother hugged Vera. "And you." She drew Mary in.

Mary's throat constricted and she wanted to cry, but Eleanor piped up with an incomprehensible melody, and the moment ended with everyone laughing at the little girl's daft song.

"Put on your dress now, darling," said Mother.

Vera took the dress and combs upstairs, and Mary followed, winking at Humphrey as she went.

Mother wore an older dress that she'd often worn to church in England. She dressed it up with a string of pearls and a pretty comb in her hair. Humphrey wore gray trousers and Mother dressed the little girls in their matching frocks.

Everyone was preoccupied in trying to make the formal clothes comfortable. Eleanor flapped her dress up and down like a chorus girl, while Rachael resisted the bow around her middle being tied snugly. Humphrey scratched at the woolen waistband. Then Vera appeared on the stair. When she reached the floor and turned round, her admiring family clapped hands at the sight of her.

Vera beamed. "Do I look all right?"

"You're a picture, my darling! Come . . ." Then Mother beckoned Vera tenderly into her arms and kissed her cheek. "Let me help you with the combs."

Mother fussed for a time with Vera's hair, then casually glanced at the dress buttons to ensure none pulled at the belly region. Thankfully, Mother was at least one dress size larger than Vera and so the dress accommodated Vera's expanded form.

When the family was ready, they walked up the hill together. But as the party entered the church and saw Father, slightly stooped over the altar with paperwork in hand, their gaiety fell away.

Mary saw Mr. Robinson, tall and striking, sitting in the first pew and watched as he and Vera exchanged glances. Mary could see in Mr. Robinson's expression that he was taken with Vera's beauty, which they all knew to be obvious as well as deep. Vera, too, locked onto James Robinson's face with admiration and joy. As Humphrey took his sister's arm and walked her awkwardly between the empty pews, Mary felt an unfamiliar feeling of loss welling up inside her.

Father looked up and was clearly moved by the sight of his eldest daughter wearing her mother's fine dress. Wisps of hair framed her face. Vera's eyes danced.

James Robinson stood and approached the altar. His gray suit was slightly ill-fitting and he had an overall air of discomfort, as if he was unaccustomed to formal dress and certainly to being in church. His sandy hair, though longer than most, was combed neatly, his mustache and beard had been trimmed, and they framed his kindly face. He stood in front and to the right of Mother and Mary who sat with Rachael between them. Eleanor sat in Mother's lap. Humphrey slipped his arm away from Vera, gave her hand a reassuring squeeze, and took his place beside Mary. They looked at each other and smiled.

The ceremony was short. A song, a prayer, the vows and exchanging of simple rings, that was all. The bride and groom were solemn, then smiling, their hands clasped as if for eternity.

As Mary noticed the way James and Vera looked into each other's eyes, a knot formed in her stomach. Would Vera's new life with James include her?

The bride bade farewell to her family outside the church gate. She scooped Eleanor in her arms and kissed her chubby cheeks. The others all received hugs in turn and then Mother advanced with a congratulatory hug for her son-in-law. Her eyes welled with tears as she took James Robinson's hands in her own and said quietly, "Take good care of her."

"I will," he said. "I know what a fine person she is." He hugged her in return.

"Now I can have your bit of the bed!" called Rachael.

Vera laughed. "Yes, Rachael, you can have my bit of the bed."

"I'll be by with your things, Vere!" said Humphrey as he turned and raced down the hill toward home, eager to spring his lanky body from the confines of his clothes and looking very much like the effort of running might very likely split the seams. Rachael skipped off behind him.

Then Father appeared out the church doors and advanced into the dappled sunlight. He went first to James, extending his hand. "I wish you well," he said, as though he were trying to convince himself of it.

"Thank you, sir," replied James Robinson. He tugged at his beard.

"She's my eldest," he began, and it was clear that he had more to say but was overcome by the moment and stopped for a time. He seemed so old standing there before the upright young man. And he seemed gray to the bone—his suit, his hair, his teeth and skin. His face was lined with time and trouble, his brow knit with worry. Father was a pitiable character at this instant, as he searched his head for words and his heart for explanation, and maybe a little consolation.

Mary thought this was her opportunity to speak. "Congratulations!" she said, in a more celebratory tone than she'd intended, considering Father.

Mr. Robinson gave Mary a hug and passed her on to Vera, who burst into sobs as soon as she was in her sister's arms.

"I'll miss you," said Mary.

"Me, too."

And there they stood, stooped and leaning against each other in the early summer sun. There can be no worse feeling, thought Mary, than holding onto someone you love and knowing that eventually you must let go.

"Goodbye," said Mary.

Vera wiped the tears from her eyes and held her sister's hands. "It's *not* goodbye," she said. "We'll see each other a good deal . . . you'll come every day if you like."

Mary had a huge lump in her throat. "I know." She smiled as best she could, then bit her lip, turned, and raced off toward home.

Mary ran straight to the barn and didn't look back. She flung herself down on the straw beside the cows and cried into her drawn-up knees. Mary sobbed with her whole chest, until she was so tired with the strain of it that the tears just stopped coming and she let go of her knees, limply looking at nothing in particular.

Then she heard giggles ringing through the air as the little girls approached the house with Mother. Chores would still need doing. The cows should go out. But then it came—the long, sharp note of Father's whistle, calling Nell from the woods.

"Nell!" she heard him shout. "Come, Nell!"

Mary's idle staring ceased and her eyes shut tight. Images of Vera, James, Father, Mother, and Mary tumbled around and around as though they were muddled up in a clothes dryer, warm and soft, turning over and over until they'd absorbed all the heat possible. She began to feel the weight of her limbs, her muscles straining to stretch, and a sure sense of herself, weary and weathered, but present right now. *She was back.*

She opened her eyes and tugged the pink quilt up to her chin. She'd been in that place again. *Bircher.* Although she was lying in her bed, she felt confident that she had not been dreaming. What was happening to Mary was much more of a descent. She could recall the feeling of falling, of slipping, twirling, turning down and down, and losing the feeling in her body. It was as though the more she grappled to resist, the faster she lost control, the sooner her mind became one with . . . with what? *With whom?* With Grandad's sister, *Mary*—her namesake. That was it. It was as though her earthly body remained of this world and her soul, her consciousness, was transferred to *the other Mary.*

Chapter Fourteen

When she awoke the next morning, Hester's bed was made. Mary swung her feet to the floor and stared at the objects on the bedside table: the photos, the arrowhead, and the whistle.

Mary touched the arrowhead, cool and smooth. She stared at the photos, forcing herself to make sense of something the way one tries to remember a phone number. But it wouldn't come because she was trying too hard, pressing herself to sort out her uneasy feelings.

She stared at the carpet under her feet, the thoroughly modern, soft, rose pink carpet. She blinked and looked again, half expecting to see a wood floor. She put the arrowhead back on the table and still sitting, divided her hair in two and began to braid one side. It was just the way . . . it was the way *Mary* braided her hair.

Mary felt bewildered, but not frightened. This wasn't a nightmare with fearful images sweeping her along out of control. The dream she was having, or the place she knew, was familiar and fine. It was odd, but not scary, often uncomfortable, sometimes sad. There was great joy in the simplicity of life. And it was the whistle that had not only an attraction, but also a power to somehow bring the past alive with vivid dreams.

Mary dressed and went downstairs. Grandad and Hester were lingering over coffee in the dining room. "We didn't want to wake you," said Hester as she pushed her chair from the table and went to the kitchen.

"You old lazybones," said Grandad, winking at Mary. "I've already been out for my ten K run."

Mary rolled her eyes and sat at the place set for her. "Right, Grandad."

Hester brought a warm plate of scrambled eggs and toast from the oven and set it in front of Mary. "Can you imagine your grandfather out for a run with those black spandex thinga-majiggers on?"

Mary was hungry and ate with barely a glance up. When she was finished, she shifted the cutlery on her plate to the side and asked, "Did you have a dog when you were growing up, Grandad?"

He looked at her over his bifocals. "Several," he said.

Mary wiped her mouth with a cloth napkin. "What were their names?"

"Clipper, Anna, Jock," he paused, thinking. "Isobel."

Mary drank the last of her juice. "That's it?" To her surprise, she felt a sense of relief.

"And of course my favorite dog, Nellie."

Mary flushed. "Nellie?" Her heart began to pound. "Nell?"

He smiled. "Yes, we did call her Nell."

The answer hit Mary like a punch in the stomach. She was speechless. If she told them she was entering another time, witnessing past events, they'd send her straight home, suspecting some manifestation of homesickness. And then would it all end? Mary stared at the pattern of her plate, the pretty fruits round the rim. *What should she do?* She was dreaming Grandad's life. This was *not* normal, but they'd never believe her.

Hester interrupted Mary's thoughts. "We saw the otters this morning, and your mother called."

Grandad poured coffee first in Hester's cup and then in his own. Mary didn't like coffee but her senses drank in the ritual of it—the strong aroma and the steam rising from the pretty teacups.

Mary pushed away from the table, relieved to have an excuse to leave. "I better call Mum."

Dad answered and Mary felt relief at his familiar voice.

"Kip made fifty bucks babysitting."

"Wow."

"Doris misses you and has taken to sleeping on *our* bed. She's developed a drooling habit."

"She's always drooled."

"Well, it's worse."

"Sorry, Dad."

"I'm not finished. She's been licking the butter."

"Doris?"

"No . . . Mum."

Mary laughed. "That's gross."

"Jean came by the other day wondering when you'd be back."

"Did you tell her?"

"Yeah." Dad paused. "We sure miss you around here."

"I miss you, too." Mary felt weak in the knees. "Dad, I . . ."

"What?"

"I . . ."

"Spit it out."

Mary came to her senses. "I was just going to say Aunt Hester really needs me here. She says I'm a big help."

Dad laughed. "I'll bet you are. Mum told me all about how helpful you are with the dog!"

Mary talked to her Mum and Kip before hanging up. She found Grandad and Hester still in the dining room. They looked up and smiled at her in such an adoring way that Mary felt momentarily startled. "Can I take Jester to the beach?"

"Capital idea," said Grandad. He twitched his mustache from side to side, tugged at the bottom of his sweater vest, then gave the okay for Jester to get up and leave with Mary.

They raced down the path to the beach, Jester plunging into the water. Mary searched for a suitable stick and swung it with all her might.

They stayed at the beach for over an hour, Jester in the water, Mary dabbling about the tidal pools, dipping her fingers into the warmed water, sending sculpins darting from fissure to seaweed.

Often and always after a hiatus from stick shredding, Jester came bounding after Mary and invariably shook as close to her as possible. Or when she wasn't expecting it, he'd suddenly appear and splash into the tidal pool.

"You're *killing* everything!" she shrieked, dragging his sopping body out of the pool while trying to find a sizable stick to distract him.

But as the morning heated up, Mary abandoned her classification of periwinkles and crabs.

She found Grandad asleep on the patio, in the shade of the umbrella. As usual, the paper lay flat across his chest. Hester was in the kitchen making a ginger loaf.

"That smells yummy," said Mary, as she slid off her sandals at the door and set them on the mat.

"Fresh ginger," said Hester, "has healing properties. Perfect for your Grandad."

"Can I help?" asked Mary, washing her hands.

"I'd love it." Hester handed her the beaters. "This needs to be smooth. No lumps."

Hester was the type who got everyone helping in the kitchen. It seemed there was always something to do, in an unhurried kind of way. It wasn't like at home when Mum was baking and while she was baking the phone rang and she talked on the phone while she was feeding the dog and then watered all the plants while the cake was in the oven and so much was going on at the same time. With Aunt Hester, baking was baking. It was peaceful.

While the ginger cake baked, Aunt Hester and Mary sat on the patio, gazing out to sea. They strained to see whether the slight movement beside the rock was an otter or a deadhead. Then the rounded spine and tail tip disappeared beneath the surface, proof positive of an otter.

"They're back," said Grandad, staring through binoculars strung around his neck. "Thank God."

"What do you mean?" asked Mary.

"A chap down the road wants to trap them," said Grandad. "He says they make a mess of his swimming pool."

"But this is their home!" said Mary indignantly.

"He thinks his pool's more important."

"Some people are horrid," said Aunt Hester.

Grandad put his hand on Mary's shoulder. "Mary, let's you and I sneak along the beach one night and see if he's put any traps out."

Mary was surprised. "Sure!"

Aunt Hester stared disapprovingly at Grandad.

"I don't like this one bit," said Aunt Hester as she trailed Grandad and Mary down to the beach. "What if that daft man shoots at you or something?"

"Come on, Mary," said Grandad, ignoring his niece. He took the stairs slowly on his crutches. "Turn on your flashlight."

Aunt Hester put her hand on Mary's shoulder. "Watch your step—it's low tide and the rocks are slippery there . . . I told Nora that I'd take care of her, Humphrey. I don't approve of this."

"Don't worry," said Mary, turning on her flashlight. "I'll watch out for him."

At the bottom of the stairs, Grandad sat awkwardly with his socked foot resting on the stones. He turned his light on Mary, who walked carefully, shining her flashlight before her.

Mary was eager to find the trap. The thought of one of her beloved otters spinning in panicked circles in the confines of a cage made her blood boil. She shone the light along the high tide mark and above it, first illuminating the stones, and then the cattails, grass, thimbleberry and salal spilling over a low cliff ledge. As she drew her light along the underbrush, she caught sight of a gap where a trap had been wedged.

She dragged the trap from the bushes, gripped the wire top with one hand, and returned to her Grandad with a trophy and a grin. "Where should we put this awful thing?"

"In the garage," said Grandad, rising now and adjusting his crutches under his armpits.

Aunt Hester directed the light onto the steps where Grandad walked. "He'll be hopping mad when he finds the traps missing. There'll be hell to pay. What if he comes over here and asks questions?"

She hurried them into the garage where they slid the trap under Grandad's workbench.

Jester barked in the kitchen, indignant at being excluded from the excursion.

"I hope you weren't seen," said Aunt Hester. "Because what you just did is steal someone's private property."

Grandad rushed to Mary's defense. "I would've done it myself if I didn't have this damn thing on my leg." Aunt Hester glowered at Grandad. "This *annoying* thing on my leg," he corrected. "Sometimes we have to take matters into our own hands. Any fool can get a trap and sell what he catches to the zoo."

Hester steadied her nerves by heating milk on the stove. Grandad hobbled into the house through the back door. He slid off his jacket and shoe, and rested on a kitchen stool.

"When I was in Hong Kong many years ago, on Lantau Island, I went into a restaurant in the middle of nowhere, where the owners had tied a monkey on a short chain," said Grandad. "She paced one way, then another, back and forth. The music was dreadful. The staff was disagreeable. I couldn't bear watching her, yet I couldn't take my eyes off her. I didn't know what kind of monkey she was, but I could tell she was unusually thin and she paced on a filthy piece of carpeting. She didn't have any water, only a rubber toy hanging from the ceiling. I ordered a fruit plate, and while the waiter placed the order with the cook, I leaned over and unclipped the chain around the monkey's neck. She leaped off the table and disappeared into the forest. I put the fruit in my napkin, settled the bill, and left the restaurant. I walked some distance, then stared for some time into the forest, hoping I might see her happily swinging from the trees. Of course, I didn't. But I flung the fruit as far into the forest as I could and I hoped for the best. I figured a little freedom was better than a cruel and monotonous existence."

They moved quietly to the chairs by the window and drank their cocoa in contemplative silence. Grandad's story had made them feel the rightness of what they'd done. Mary felt a sense of connectedness to this facet of her family. She realized that the sense of justice she felt, her own rules of right and wrong, seemed to belong to Grandad as well.

She went into the kitchen to get the cookie tin. When she returned, she found Aunt Hester leaning closer to Grandad.

"Uncle Humphrey," said Aunt Hester. "You know that Mummy would love it here."

Grandad's whiskers turned downwards like a schnauzer.

Aunt Hester's voice grew charmingly soft. "You must forgive yourself and see Mummy again. She's longing to see *you*."

Forgive yourself? Mary slid her hand into her pocket and felt the whistle. She suddenly remembered when she'd first seen Grandad in the hospital and he'd clutched her hand so desperately. *I never meant any harm.*

Chapter Fifteen

The next morning when Mary awoke, she was alone in the room as usual. She dressed and found Grandad and Aunt Hester in the dining room.

"There you are," said Aunt Hester as she pushed away from the table and gave Mary a squeeze around the shoulders. "Pancakes?"

"Thank you," said Mary as she slid onto a chair.

Grandad seemed subdued this morning. He winked at her, and quietly finished his breakfast. "Tonight, we should check to see if the scoundrel's baited another trap."

"Oh, Uncle Humphrey," said Aunt Hester, "is this really the right thing to do with your granddaughter?"

Grandad peered at Aunt Hester over his reading glasses. "Of course it's right." He poured coffee for both of them.

Mary remembered the first time she'd seen the otters five years ago. She and Grandad were playing bocce ball on the lawn when they looked up and saw the sleek forms frisking their way to the big rock—one curved back, then another and another, all followed by the pointy tail tips. Breaking the surface with sleak faces and climbing the slope with such an elated gait, *tarump . . . tarump . . . tarump* to the grassy top, the otters rolled in something unseen, crab shells maybe, then back to the ocean effortlessly, playfully weaving their bodies around marine obstacles until they disappeared from sight.

Mary put her cutlery together on the side of her plate. "What if he catches us?"

Aunt Hester raised her eyebrows.

"We're too crafty for that," said Grandad.

Mary smiled. "Operation Otter Trap!" Then she polished off the rest of her orange juice.

The day passed quietly. Jester expected his walk after breakfast, as usual. If too much time elapsed between breakfast and walk, he'd find one of Grandad's shoes and bring it to him.

"Take it to her," Grandad said, pointing at Mary.

After the walk, Mary usually took Jester to the beach for a swim. Then she'd dry him off in his little room and leave him to sleep off the rest of the morning while she helped Aunt Hester in the kitchen. It surprised Mary just how much thought went into meal planning. Hester often said things like, "Shall we have beans or peas for the green vegetable?" and "Which would you rather with the fish . . . rice or potatoes?"

Mum simply plucked a bunch of things from the fridge and threw them all together under the general heading of Stew. Autumn Vegetable Stew. Spring Stew. Winter Stew. Moroccan Stew. And Mary's least favorite, the dreaded Marinated Tofu Stew. Mary remembered a grade two project when she had to write favorite and least favorite foods in her journal. Under the category of least favorite, Mary wrote in bold black letters *STEW* and underlined it with all twelve of her colored markers. After this not so subtle clue, Mum began adding alphabet pasta to the stew.

After lunch, Grandad and Hester collapsed in the big living room chairs for a rest. Hester's eyes closed only briefly, while Grandad napped for at least an hour. While they rested, Mary often wandered about the house. This house had no clutter, had a place for everything and everything placed just so. Most horizontal surfaces, all the antiques everywhere were dustless and decorated with the simplest of things—a single glass vase with flowers, a lord and lady in ceramic finery, a writing folder and ink well, long dried up. Mary loved to touch these objects, to look inside, to read the book titles in the den, to feel the velvety drapes. She loved the smell of the chesterfields, the chairs, and the blankets. After nap-time, the three generations sat on the porch with glasses of Grandad's favorite, queer tasting lime cordial. On clear, sunny days, they'd play bocce ball on the lawn, or croquet, then pull out their paints and try again to record the waves just right or capture a seagull on the rock. When the wind picked up, as it so often did on the water, they played *Spellicans* or cards in the living room. On a couple of rainy days, Grandad found a puzzle in his den and they spilled the tiny pieces onto the dining room table and worked on fitting together a mare and her foal in the English countryside. Unlike home, where someone was either listening to the radio or the stereo, or watching TV, the only sound aside from their voices was the grandfather clock in the hallway and the click click click of Jester's toenails on the linoleum floor in the kitchen.

After game time, as Hester called it, Grandad settled back into his chair to read while Mary and Aunt Hester put on the tea. And this wasn't just a mug of tea like Mum had at home. This was the teapot, teaspoons, three cups and saucers, and a plate of biscuits, pound cake, and bird's nest cookies. This they ate at the round table in the living room, often in silence, punctuated only by satisfied *mmm*'s and grins and sometimes, "I can't resist another one of these."

After dinner, there was much impatience as they waited for the plodding sun to sink behind the evergreens in the west. When darkness finally fell over the countryside, Mary sprang from her chair with flashlight in hand, offering the other to her Grandad.

They looked into each other's eyes and chorused, "Operation Otter Trap!"

"Hurrah!" added Grandad.

"Lunatics," groaned Aunt Hester.

Although it was early summer, the night was cool from the breeze off the water.

Suddenly, they heard a scampering sound and then a black streak shot past them on the beach. Jester! Mary thrust her free hand into her pocket and grabbed the whistle. Without thinking, she pulled it out and blew into it. She turned toward Grandad, her head swimming. Mary fell to the ground.

She was off, moving dizzyingly through the airy space with her eyes closed. She tried not to panic, knowing what was ahead of her. There was no feeling now, and her heart had maintained a steady beat, enough to help her reach the other body, blend with it and let the quiet seep into her soul.

Mary looked up from her misery and gazed into Humphrey's eyes.

"You," he said, as he sat in the straw beside his sister, "could use a little cheering up." He held out his hand for Mary to grasp. "We'll take Vera her things together."

Mary looked down. "Oh, Humphrey, what are we to do without Vera? I can't imagine how it will be without her."

"She's only married! She's not dead!" He looked sidelong at his sister and she tried a smile. "She won't be far through the woods, and just think—it'll give us a new place to go and get away from Father!"

Mary burst out laughing and hugged her brother. "Oh, Humphrey," she sniffed. "Whatever would I do without you?"

Chapter Sixteen

They gathered Vera's bags together, the ones she'd packed the night before and left at the foot of the bed.

"Mind you get all the things she's left about the house," said Mother. "Vera can be forgetful when she sets her mind to it."

They retrieved her coat from the coat hooks, her brush from beside the mirror, combs and ribbons in a woven basket, and a pair of black boots from beside the door.

"Tell her I'll be 'round with bread," said Mother, "and a pot of soup. I'll get it started when Eleanor naps." She kissed her daughter's sweet-smelling head.

Father strode down the hill and into the house.

"I'm giving the dog to Vera," he said as he put a piece of wood in the stove.

"To Vera?" Humphrey asked.

"Right," said Father. "A familiar face might ease the transition. I thought the little girls might be upset, but I've found a litter and secured a pup."

"Why is Nellie going to Vera's new house?" asked Rachael who had overheard part of the conversation. Her lower lip quivered.

Father crouched down to Rachael's level. "Remember the puppy you met at church several weeks ago?"

Rachael nodded.

"Mrs. McDiuhi is selling her." Father sat down on his old chair beside the fire and pulled Rachael onto his lap. "I've said we'll buy her if you'd like and she could be our new dog. You can even name her if you can think of something sensible."

Rachael shrieked with joy. "When? When? When? When?"

Father stroked his beard. "Perhaps Humphrey could pick her up on the way home from Vera's new house."

Rachael jumped off his lap and skipped around the house. Eleanor struggled in Mother's arms, desperate to be part of the excitement even though she didn't quite know what the excitement was all about.

Humphrey took up Nell's leash. "We'll be off then."

Now Mary was the eldest girl in the family home. She helped Mother more in the kitchen, learning to bake bread from start to finish. She refined her embroidery and used her first project to cover a footstool. She helped more with Rachael and Eleanor, bathing them, feeding them, and watching them when Mother did her own chores. She'd never quite realized the extent of Vera's responsibilities.

Mary didn't mind. The activity kept her from missing Vera too much. Only at night, when she slid into bed beside Rachael, did she miss the whispered conversations with her older sister. Yes, there was more room in the bed, but she longed to feel Vera's body beside her own.

It wasn't as if Mary never saw her sister. In fact, she visited almost every day, forging a footpath between the jack pines and cottonwoods from her house to Vera's. Father insisted that Humphrey accompany his sister. There were wild animals in the woods, coyotes and bears.

It took about twenty minutes to walk there, ten to run the distance. James was often out working, or busy painting, so the sisters would sit on the small porch steps and talk. Sometimes they'd walk into the orchard behind the house and weave through the trees, sizing up the ripening fruit, and other times they'd walk to the lakeshore picking fat blackberries. Humphrey often dared them to throw the berries in the air so he might catch them in his mouth. More often than not, hysterical laughter would follow when he missed the mark and the fruit plopped like a purple bird-dropping on his forehead or nose.

To Mary's amazement, Vera's belly grew larger and tighter. Often when they were out walking, they stopped and talked and laid their hands on Vera's stomach. It would take a minute for the baby to notice the walking and rocking had stopped. Then the kicking would start, and they'd giggle and guess— was it a hand or a foot or an elbow? And always, one of them would say, "I can't believe it!" And another would say, "I wonder what it'll be." Then they'd all guess boy or girl and roar with laughter over possible names.

"Eunice!" shouted Mary, "After dear Mrs. Saymer!"

"Brown Betty!" suggested Humphrey, "After Pitfield's horse!"

"Ronald!" shouted Vera, "After Lord Talbot's perfect son!"

But the time would come for Mary and Humphrey to leave. They'd all thread through the trees to the cabin and catch their breath on the porch steps, where Mary and Humphrey bid Vera good-bye with hugs and kisses.

August was like a Sunday. The crispness of each morning and evening was the sign of summer's end, and each day came faster than the one before, tossing them all into autumn before they knew it. By September, the leaves were on fire—reds, yellows, oranges—lighting up the sky until they were tugged from their branches by the playful wind.

Humphrey and Mary tossed handfuls of leaves into the air above Rachael and Eleanor's arms, stretching skyward like cornstalks, trying to catch them but loving them slipping through their fingers.

School started for the three oldest children, while Eleanor waved goodbye on the porch.

"Take care of Isobel," instructed Rachael, as she patted her growing-up pup on the head. "Mind she doesn't chew any boots up."

Eleanor laughed and tugged at the puppy's ears, just as another puppy would do. Isobel rolled on her back, exposing the white splash on her belly that flowed like a stream up to her chin.

Mary borrowed books from school for Vera. Novels mostly, but she also found a book about famous painters. James liked that one, too, and he and Vera, Mary, and Humphrey took turns reading it, marveling at the exotic lives of the impressionists.

Father visited rarely, and when he did, it was for practical reasons like delivering firewood. Along the path he'd come with the wooden wheelbarrow; then he and James would stack it. Sometimes he brought cream from Miss Milk or a fresh piece of fish he'd caught in the lake. Their conversations were brief, if anything. James wanted to thank him for his help and once put a comforting hand on his father-in-law's back. But the old man moved quickly out of reach and so James never tried again.

Mother visited, too, always with food under her arm. An enormous kettle of soup lasted the week. Kept frozen on the back porch, James hacked off a section to warm on the stove. The little girls brought biscuits and bread, while Isobel, leggy and lively, contributed the entertainment.

Rachael was delighted about the baby. She was one of the few people in the family who regularly commented about the impending birth.

"Can't wait for our new baby," she'd blurt out as she pointed to Vera's rounded form. "Who's hiding in there!"

Eleanor was almost two, now, and didn't deeply understand what was going on. Her world was pretty much unchanged, as play, sleep, and food followed one after the other as reliably as night follows day.

The girls loved visiting Vera's house, a new destination that was fun and familiar. They grew less shy with their brother-in-law. He took them easily by the hand down to the creek where they threw in dry leaves and watched them tumble through the current and into the lake.

James took several caretaking jobs for wealthy landowners who rarely worked and often went off to polo matches, cricket games, and fox hunts. On these jobs, he took the girls along to watch as he tended the animals. He piled Rachael and Eleanor into the hay barrow and wove about the yard, pretending to tip them over into the steaming piles of manure. The little girls were breathless with giggling, begging for more when James ceased his clowning.

When it rained, or a cold wind blew outside, James often sat the girls at the kitchen table and gave them each a piece of paper and dabs of paint to make their own pictures.

"I have some little thing in the house to remind me of everyone," said Vera, as she propped the masterpieces on her kitchen windowsill.

Vera's stomach was as round as a full moon, the skin as hard as a tennis ball. Her clothes were uncomfortable and hot. Her legs were swollen and at least once a day she had terrible heartburn.

"I've got to get up for the toilet two or three times in the night," she confided to Mary. "I'm worn out."

Mary must've told mother because on her next trip through the trail, she bustled into the kitchen, rolled up her sleeves, and set to cleaning the place. Mary helped, and together they made the cabin sparkle while Vera slept.

When she awoke, Rachael and Eleanor were cutting out paper snowflakes by the wood stove. Outside the window, snow fell fast, nature's announcement that a long and very cold winter had begun.

Father, Humphrey, James, and Mr. Wilks spent the afternoon cutting ice blocks from the Kootenay River. They piled them on Wilks' sleigh pulled by his team of horses and delivered them to neighboring icehouses. When that was done, they set to work constructing one of their own, packing several feet of sawdust inside to trap the cold.

With the snow carpeting the front porch, Mary secretly worried about the trail from their house to Vera's house. How would they keep it open throughout the winter? What if they couldn't get through when the baby came?

Chapter Seventeen

On the morning of December third, James raced through the woods to report that Vera had been up in the night with a cramping belly.

"I believe the baby may be coming," he said with ashen lips. Then he turned tail and ran immediately back to the cottage.

Mary tumbled down the stairs, tugging her leggings on as quickly as she could. Mother dashed to the porch for her boots and laced them up.

Father and the little girls stood on the porch. "Send word," he said, "as soon as possible." Humphrey slipped a flint arrowhead into his pocket. He'd found it embedded in glacial sand during his first week in Canada. He hoped it'd be a good luck charm.

Mother grasped a shawl around her shoulders. Mary wore a coat. Their breath puffed out of their mouths and noses like oxen, as they struggled through the snow. Mary heard James calling as they were almost upon the house.

"Thank God," he said, as he saw them appear. "*Please* hurry."

Through the door they heard Vera, sobbing and saying, "Mother, help me, *please* . . . "

Mary's eyes widened and she felt stricken when she saw Vera lying on her side. Her mouth was gaping wide, her lips pale and shapeless. She had a pillow between her knees and a light blanket draped over her body. Beside her on the bed was a hot water bottle, and on the table, a glass of water and a thermometer.

Mother walked straight to Vera and took her hand in her own. "I'm here now," said Mother. Then Mary and James watched as Mother put her face only inches from Vera's. "I'm here, dear, and it's time for the baby to be born and everything will be all right."

Mother spoke clearly and loudly, as if Vera had a hearing deficit. It made Mary anxious.

James paced. "What should we do? Should we take her to the Kootenay Lake Hospital?"

Mother drenched a facecloth in warm water and wrung it out. "How long has she been like this?"

James looked panicked, looked as if he couldn't recall anything. "In the night," he said. "That's when she started to have the pains." He paused. "But they weren't much and when she lay down, they'd stop. We thought it wasn't real."

Suddenly Vera curled forward and shrieked.

James stood startled as Vera gripped Mother's hand so tightly that her own hand turned white. Mary watched as the grip lessened and then her hand fell away.

James continued. "We both fell asleep and Vera woke up suddenly in pain." He paused. "Is there something I can do?"

"We'll see the baby born today," said Mother. "But we must remain calm so we can help Vera through this." Mother looked pointedly at Mary. "Fetch Mrs. Fairclough, tell her Vera's having contractions, and she must come right away. Ask her to ring Dr. Cathcart first and have him come as soon as possible." Mother looked down at Vera and stroked her hair. "Tell them there's a path cleared from the church to our house and from our house to here. If they try to come on the wagon road, it'll take twice as long." Mother looked up at Mary. "Take Nell with you."

Mary wrapped Mother's shawl around her shoulders and slipped out the door. Snow fell easily, despite the whirling world in Mary's mind. She wondered for the first time whether it was possible that Vera could die, as Dorothy Fry had died in childbirth. Mary ran faster, tugging on Nell's leash. She tripped on the length of her own skirts.

"Damn this bloody frock!" she said out loud. "Damn. Damn. Damn." And once this frustration slipped from her lips, she started to cry, the warm tears a relief from the chill on her face. "God, don't let her die. *Don't* let her die. *Don't* let her die." Her chanting and footsteps beat a rhythm in the snow and in the air and in her head.

Mary reached the wagon road, which had thankfully seen some traffic on it in the morning. She ran where the wheels had compacted the snow, around the tree stumps, until she came to Mrs. Fairclough's house at the end of a long, straight driveway. But before she reached the front door, Mrs. Fairclough burst from the door with a bag in her hand.

"Humphrey told me," she started in her Scottish lilt. "Came a few minutes ago, so I've called Dr. Cathcart who'll be afoot already."

Then she and Mary and Nell turned and raced back along the wagon road.

"Mother said to go along the church path," panted Mary.

"Six of one, half a dozen of the other," said Mrs. Fairclough. "But I'm sure your mother knows best." Then Mrs. Fairclough's feet went out from underneath her and she fell hard on her bottom. "Bloody hell!" Then she glanced up at Mary, ashamed.

Mary stretched out her hand. "I've sworn myself this morning . . . twice," she smiled.

They laughed together and pushed onward, through the pines and snow to the little house in the woods.

When they opened the door, Mary was startled by the blast of heat from the stove that James seemed to be nervously stoking. She and Mrs. Fairclough bustled into the bedroom where Vera was kneeling on the bed now, wearing only her long undershirt. One of her arms was draped over Dr. Cathcart, who stood beside the bed. The other arm was draped around Mother who kneeled beside her. Blood spattered the bed beneath her.

"Push *now!*" said Dr. Cathcart, who'd given his position to Mrs. Fairclough, so he could tend to the baby.

Vera groaned again, loud and long. Mary stood on the other side of Dr. Cathcart and said quietly, "I'm here now, Vere. I can't wait to see the baby." She swallowed the tremendous lump in her throat.

Mother's full attention was on Vera. "You're doing *very* well, darling. Very, very well."

And as if as an exclamation mark, Vera let out another groan, with her eyes closed, her face splotchy and moist.

"There's the head," said Dr. Cathcart calmly.

Mary gasped. "It really *is* a head!"

"Better than the feet," said Mrs. Fairclough. "I've seen enough of the feet coming first."

Mother glared at Mrs. Fairclough who looked admonished.

Vera tried to collapse backwards, but Mrs. Fairclough and Mother held onto her firmly. "I can't do this any longer," she pleaded.

"Yes, you can," said Mother. "You're doing a magnificent job, dear. Soon we'll know whether it's a boy or a girl."

"I have to push again?" said Vera weakly, and with that, Vera screwed up her face, and pushed. A small set of bloody shoulders, first one, then the other, appeared. Dr. Cathcart's huge hands encased the little being as the rest slid out slowly, smothered in sticky wetness and blood.

"It's a wee lass!" said Mrs. Fairclough, who melted with the moment.

Mother and Mrs. Fairclough eased Vera down onto her back.

"James!" called Mother through the closed door. "It's a girl!" Then she turned back to her daughter. "Well done, darling."

Dr. Cathcart cut the umbilical cord and passed the screaming newborn to Mrs. Fairclough. She took hold of her in a clean sheet and swaddled her gently before passing the baby into Vera's arms.

"Hold her for a wee moment, dear," said Mrs. Fairclough. "The doctor'll check her over while you deliver the placenta."

Vera looked surprised. "I have to deliver that, *too*?"

"It won't hurt," said Mother. "Just push it out."

Dr. Cathcart inspected the baby while Mary watched Vera prepare to deliver the placenta. A great, red and beige blob of a thing appeared on the bed sheets.

"My God," said Mary, startled by its appearance.

Vera reached out her arms for the baby and took the newborn warmly to her breast, smelling in the scent of what was hers, seemingly swelled by emotion.

Mother opened the door and there stood James, his jaw hung open like a drunkard. His eyes widened as he surveyed the scene. Their bedroom was a mess of bloody sheets and pots of warm water. Mrs. Fairclough was collecting the medical paraphernalia together and passed the instruments to Dr. Cathcart, while Mary, Mother, and James circled the bed in joyful disbelief that this tiny creature was a new member of their world. Tears trickled down Vera's cheeks. "I'm so happy," whispered Vera. The baby yawned, and Vera stroked her soft skin. "We'll call her Hester, then, after your mother."

James nodded.

"Hester," said Dr. Cathcart, as he dried his hands on a clean towel, "is a healthy, robust little lass. Congratulations."

"Run and tell Father," said Mother to Mary. "Tell them to come." She looked down at her grandchild and stroked the baby's arm. "Tell them Hester has arrived." Then Mother's voice broke and she held her hand to her mouth.

Chapter Eighteen

Vera was asleep when Father, Humphrey, and the girls arrived. Mother had tidied up the birthing area. She sat at the table with a strong cup of tea, watching James cradle Hester in the armchair before the fire.

"We heard the news," whispered Father as he entered with his finger to his lips so the girls wouldn't wake their sister. There was some excitement in his voice now, some new energy. "Let's see the baby."

James tugged away a bit of blanket so Hester's face could be better seen. The eyes of the two men met for a moment, then snapped back to the baby. Father was speechless, only staring as Mother held the little girls at a distance.

Rachael was in awe, gawking at her new niece, whose every feature was so small and pink—the ears, the nose, and the perfectly formed lips. Eleanor took a quick look at the bundle and swirled off to play at the sink.

Father stoked the fire. Snow fell outside the windows as each of them welcomed baby Hester with unspoken prayers of love and long life. Except Eleanor, a mere baby herself, who after playing for a time with her twigs had crawled into Mother's lap like a kitten, and curled up to sleep.

Christmas was on them in no time, and Mary had noticed Father spending long hours writing and rewriting his sermon. On many nights, the little light from the church shone until she blew out her own lamp and went to sleep.

School let out for a brief holiday. Humphrey, Mary, and Rachael spent hours throwing snowballs at each other, making snowmen and angels. Eleanor played in short spurts, regularly complaining of cold hands and feet. The dogs frisked about in the snow, catapulting themselves through the deeper drifts and launching themselves at each other.

Vera didn't leave the house much, as she worried she might fall in the woods and injure the baby. Only on Christmas Day, she and James, carrying baby Hester, trudged through the trail to the church.

Mary noticed a twinkle in Father's eyes as he looked out at his congregation, sitting now in pools of cast-off woolens. She smiled at him and noticed how he spent some moments drinking in the sight of his grandchild, bundled in the arms of his eldest daughter. Mary felt warmed from the inside, peaceful and dreamy, and proud, too, of this tranquil place her father had created—a place people had chosen to meet on such a special day.

After the service, there was a buzz about the church while the women in their Christmas best hovered around the baby, delighting in her infant finery. No detail was left unspoken, from her tiny fingernails to the soft auburn hair that belonged to her mother and grandmother.

Mrs. Fairclough twice related her involvement in the birth and how she'd been the first to announce the gender of the baby. Everyone had heard this several times already, though they appeared as excited as they were on the first telling. Even some of the men stepped forward, mumbling approval in Hester's direction.

Mary reveled in this Christmas. Unlike England, which was often dark and pouring on Christmas Day, Bircher was spectacular. A recent blizzard had passed through town and left it shimmering. The mountains were wrapped in snow, the great evergreen boughs hobbled with the weight of it.

Father's church was picturesque, yet humble, small and solid, seemingly like a sanctuary in the wintry landscape. He stood in the doorway now, waving off the last of his parishioners into the white, white winter day. Mary heard them talk about Vera's Hester, about their impending meals, visiting family, frozen pipes, and drafty homes. Yet they were happy and smiling, uplifted by community and by Christmas itself. Mary found herself thinking that she had not seen Father looking so pleasant and rested in quite some time.

When the last of the faithful had disappeared down the wagon road, it was time to head home for the rest of the Christmas celebration. James fed the roaring fire while the family assembled for present opening.

Mother had sewn dolls for Eleanor, Rachael, and Hester.

"My *boomers!*" squealed Eleanor, when she realized that her old blue bloomers had been used to fashion the doll's apron.

"My worn winter frock!" Rachael shrieked, as she made the same discovery on her own doll.

Humphrey unwrapped a slingshot Father had made. Tied to the wooden Y-frame was a small piece of rubber from a bicycle inner tube with a leather pouch fashioned from the tongue of Humphrey's old shoe.

"Capital!" said Humphrey, as he tugged at the rubber strip, closing one eye as if to make a shot. "I can play with the chaps at the mill!"

"I saw them in the fall," said Mary. "They'd found a great log with annular rings and a central pith perfect for the bull's eye."

"I expect you could compete with the best of them now," said Father. As he smiled, his lined face lit up.

Vera and Mary unwrapped flannel nightdresses made by Mother. She'd used the remainder to make a miniature replica for Hester.

"They're beautiful," exclaimed Vera, holding up Hester's nightdress for everyone to see.

Father handed a present to his wife.

"We haven't money for this sort of thing, Rudyard," she said with a teasing smile.

"No money, no money, no money," chanted Rachael, tugging the clothes off her doll so she could examine what was underneath. "We haven't got no money!"

"*Any* money, darling," said Mother.

"We haven't got any money, darling," repeated Rachael, totally distracted now with the muslin underthings on her doll. "You will be Alice." She looked directly at the doll's stitched eyes. "Say your name." Rachael moved the doll up and down and said, "I am Alice."

Then Mother unwrapped a beautiful wooden bowl.

"I bought it from an Indian," said Father. "A rather nice fellow. He's put his initials on the underside."

Mother turned the bowl over and they all marveled at the smoothness of it.

"Thank you, Rudyard," she said. "It's lovely."

Then Mary handed Vera a package. "For Hester," she said. "My favorite niece."

Vera beamed, as any mother does who finds her baby surrounded by love. She carefully untied the string to find a small stuffed cat.

"I made it," said Mary, "from my old sundress."

"I remember!" exclaimed Vera. "I can't believe you saved it from so long ago."

"I thought I could make doll's clothes with it," said Mother. "Mary found it in my sewing trunk and decided it would be perfect for Hester's first toy."

"Oh, it is!" said Vera, who examined the little cat made of a blue and green paisley print and sewn up the sides with small, perfect blanket stitches. Black eyes and nose were sewn with embroidery thread that was also used for little drooping whiskers. Vera leaned the little cat against her daughter as she slept.

Lastly, Humphrey handed Vera a small present wrapped in a handkerchief. "It's for Hester," he said.

Vera unwrapped Humphrey's good luck charm, the flint arrowhead he'd put in his trousers pocket the day Hester was born.

"Oh, Humphrey," said Vera, "this was *your* special keepsake."

"I believe it'll keep Hester safe from harm," he said. "I want her to have it."

Father rose and went to his dresser. He pulled the British flag from a soft pouch, placed it on the floor and unfolded it. Then he stood with it in his outstretched arms.

Everyone clapped as he fixed it to the banister.

Chapter Nineteen

Mary was astonished to see how quickly Hester grew. By springtime, as the glacial streams thundered into the well-treed valleys and new pale leaves unfurled and stretched their fresh tips like cats' claws, Hester was sitting up unassisted, banging on pots with a wooden spoon. She began to eat pureed vegetables and homemade applesauce. Rachael found great enjoyment spooning food into Hester's open mouth, which yawned wide like a baby robin waiting for worms.

For Hester to remain strong boned and healthy, Mr. Wilks sporadically popped around with a fresh pitcher of milk from his herd. It was purportedly the richest milk in the valley with the greatest amount of cream crowning the surface.

Humphrey and Mary visited almost daily. Very often, Mary simply occupied the baby while Vera got on with her domestic duties. Humphrey willingly helped with the cottage maintenance and jobs at neighboring farms.

James treated Humphrey and Mary as if they were already grown up, engaging in interesting conversation and sharing his treasured paints and papers with them. The three of them often walked to a picturesque spot in the forest or clearing with a good view of the mountains, and painted together. James was a considerate teacher, intervening only when necessary and quick to praise.

On wet days, they'd often sit inside and paint a bowl of fruit or try quick sketches of Hester.

"The empire's at war!" Humphrey blurted through the screen door on a humid afternoon in August.

Vera swung the door open, eyes wide. "War?" She wiped her hands on her apron. "Good God!"

Mary left Hester playing on the floor and drew closer.

"Reservists are scrambling to book passage home," said Humphrey. "A newsboy showed me the extra. It said *Empire at War.*"

From then on, Humphrey brought news of the war—how many had enlisted from their area, how many were wounded and missing in action. Mrs. Fairclough's own nephew Hugh was killed at sea. Irene McCreedy's brother lost a leg and was recovering in London. Each bit of news was so hugely unfair for the families so far from the comforts of England. It was even passed around that dear Mrs. Wright had lost both of her young sons, and with her husband so ill besides.

"I can't believe it's all happening," said Mary one day as she kneaded dough at the kitchen table.

Vera nodded. "It seems impossible, doesn't it, that so many men are dying, or coming home blind and deaf?" She pulled up the washboard from under the sink.

The air was fresh with birdsong. Mary found it hard to imagine the constant din of gunfire, growing louder and more deafening and then indiscriminately killing one's friends and leaving them lying in no-man's-land to die slowly because enemy fire kept rescuers from the injured.

At night, James tirelessly painted—sweeping watercolors of the mountains and valley, the river and creek beds, whimsical sketches of Hester playing on the floor or frolicking in the tub. He painted an oil portrait of Vera in the dress she wore on her wedding day, with cherubic Hester in her lap. With no money for framing, most of the paintings lived propped against a bedroom wall or leaning on a window ledge. The larger canvases were slid under the bed.

James painted a watercolor of Reverend Mills' church, dressed in snow with a pathway shoveled to its door. Humphrey fashioned a frame of sorts and Mother hung it in the church alcove. Mrs. Dryvens, parishioner and secretary to the mayor, noticed the delicate painting and inquired of the artist. James obligingly showed her his other works and she excitedly selected four of the largest landscape canvases for display at the Bircher Museum. They would be hung for a year, she assured James, and would have affixed to them both the artist's name and a price James thought was ridiculously high. But it was kind of Mrs. Dryvens, and it was most definitely good exposure for James's talent.

Although this was immensely encouraging, having one's paintings hanging on a wall didn't support his young family. James found employment on local farms, mowing hay (often with a scythe when the horse-drawn mower broke), and performing any feats of manual labor available to him. He had a reputation for being honest and reliable, and lately he was seen as less of a recluse as his wife and daughter drew him from his shell. Many employers purchased his paintings, as he'd cleverly include their houses and barns in his landscapes. Unlike Mrs. Dryvens, he was reluctant to sell his paintings for much, as he lacked business skill and confidence.

Then came the good news. Humphrey, always the messenger and particularly at tea time, rushed over a letter for James. Mary followed with a pound cake from Mother. *James Robinson* it read on the envelope. *By hand.* James slit open the envelope with his pocket knife and pulled from it a letter. He handed it to Vera. All were silent while she read:

Dear Mr. Robinson,

We are delighted to inform you that your oil paintings recently displayed for sale in the alcove of the Bircher Museum have been purchased at full price by a Mr. and Mrs. Larry Wilmot of San Francisco, California.

The monies will be available from the secretary's office tomorrow, September 15, 1914 between the hours of 9 am and 4 pm.

We offer our hearty congratulations and wish you much success in your future endeavors.

Yours truly,

Mrs. Richard A. Dryvens

Executive Secretary, Mayor's Office

James gave a tremendous whoop of joy as he, Vera, Mary, and Humphrey laced their arms together and danced in a circle, round and round, exclaiming all the while about their incredible good fortune. At last they dropped onto kitchen chairs, chests heaving with exertion, and eagerly devoured what was now a celebratory tea.

"I'll fetch it tomorrow," said James as he ran his long fingers through his hair. "On my way home from the McLean ranch."

"Darling," said Vera, "You're seldom home before dinner from the McLeans. Do you really think you can reach the municipal office before four?"

"Right," replied James, his mind still reeling from the news.

"Perhaps *I* could fetch it," suggested Vera, "if Mary could watch Hester."

"I'm at school all day," said Mary.

"Right," said James. "We're not thinking straight."

"Why don't Mary and I just fetch the money on our way home from school?" suggested Humphrey. "It won't take long to get from the schoolhouse to the municipal hall and we could cut through Brown's fields on the way home."

They agreed this was the best plan.

"Let's not tell Father just now," suggested Vera. "Wait until we have the money in our hands to show him and he'll finally believe that you're an artist in your own right." She smiled at James. "It just goes to show that we should be asking a better price for your paintings, when there are people who want them and will pay good money for them."

Vera, Mary, and Humphrey were surely the family James had never had, and his spine grew visibly straighter as they praised his talent and his good fortune.

"Why don't we build a little artist's studio onto the house," Vera suggested. "That way, Hester won't be into your paints all the time."

"I think you and James should take a trip," Humphrey proposed. "To town perhaps, for paints and supplies and maybe something new to wear."

"I could watch Hester one evening while you have a fancy dinner out," offered Mary. "And then you could build your little studio!"

Although James relished the ideas, he insisted the money should first go into the bank. "I'm sure the time will come soon enough when we'll need it for something really important," he said.

The next day dawned with excitement. At school, Humphrey and Mary watched the clock with anticipation, to the detriment of their sums. He and Mary exchanged knowing glances. She envied her brother the exciting job of bringing the money to James and Vera, as Tuesday was her assigned day to tend the girls so mother could bottle food. But she was grateful to at least accompany her brother to the Municipal Hall before heading home.

When the schoolmistress finally rang the bell, Mary and Humphrey sprang from their seats and uncharacteristically jostled for the door. With their satchels over their shoulders, they sprang from the schoolhouse and bolted down the road.

"We were all very taken with your brother-in-law's talent," gushed the secretary.

"He's very good," Mary agreed.

Humphrey nodded.

The secretary pushed her spectacles onto the bridge of her nose as she retrieved a thick envelope from the drawer. "This is rather worrisome," she said, "such a great sum of money in an envelope."

"Why didn't the man issue a cheque?" Humphrey asked.

Mrs. Dryvens knit her brow. "We've been puzzling over it," she said. "A most unusual couple. They had motorcar trouble, you know, and there aren't many people around here who know much about motorcars. So it took some time before it was repaired. In the meantime, they dined at the hotel, walked along the river, and then wandered into the museum." She fastened the top button of her sweater. "Frances over at the museum said they were smitten with the paintings. Mr. Wilmot said it would remind him of their wonderful vacation, save the trouble over the motorcar. Then he just pulled a great lump of cash from his coat pocket, counted it out on the desk, and Frances almost fell over backwards. I suppose they had it for their travels." She lowered her voice. "They looked fairly well off with Mrs. Wilmot in diamonds and rubies and her hair so beautifully arranged."

Humphrey held the weighty envelope in his hand. He'd never felt the mass of so many bills.

Mrs. Dryvens looked distressed. "Perhaps Mr. Robinson should come himself and take it directly to the bank?"

Mary looked at Humphrey. "What do you think?"

Humphrey slipped the envelope into his satchel, buckled the catch and held it, once more, against his body. "I think they'll be disappointed if we don't come home with the money."

Mrs. Dryvens gave a terse smile. "As you wish."

Humphrey and Mary walked out the front door and down the road. Just as they'd passed the post office, Humphrey stopped.

"Father!"

"Humphrey, my boy. Mary. Where are you off to?"

Humphrey looked at Mary. "Vera's house," he said.

Father looked at him over the top of his spectacles and gestured to a street bench. "Sit down and eat this," he said, as he passed him a brown wrapping containing strips of smoked fish.

Humphrey hesitated a moment, frustrated by the delay. But, catching his father's look, he slid off his heavy satchel and sat on the bench. They each ate a strip of trout before Father stood up and said, "Wait here."

"Where are you going?"

"Post office. Shan't be a minute."

Humphrey and Mary grumbled while they ate the rest of the fish. Father returned with a letter that he slid into his coat pocket. It appeared that either the effort of retrieving the letter, or else the contents itself had siphoned the color from his face. Humphrey was too wary of his father to ask questions, and it took all his courage to simply say, "I'd best be off."

"Your mother needs flour," said Father. "Fetch it from the general store and put it on credit."

Humphrey felt thwarted. He wanted to get to James and Vera's house. "But I . . ."

Reverend Mills looked up at his son. "I need to rest for a moment. Do as you're told."

Mary felt brave. "Why don't I fetch the flour and Humphrey could push on to Vera's house?"

Rudyard Mills looked over the top of his glasses at his daughter, and Mary could see it coming. "Aren't you supposed to be helping your mother at home?" He looked away and gestured with his hand. "Off you go then, hurry up."

Mary was furious at Father. He was ruining the day, blighting the celebration. She ran as fast as she could to the church and then down the big hill to home. In an uncharacteristic bad temper, Mary went reluctantly about her duties, impatient with the little girls and scowling at the implements before her. When she was finished her chores, she asked if she might go to Vera's, then ran quickly through the woods, anticipating the excitement and feeling her mood lift.

Vera and James were standing when she entered.

"We've been pacing the floor," said Vera. "Where's Humphrey?"

"He hasn't been?" Mary was aghast.

"No," said James, Hester on his hip. "I'm already home since half past and there's no sign of him. Did you go to the hall with him?"

Just as Mary was about to answer, they heard steps on the porch.

"Humphrey!" said Vera. "Where *have* you been? We've been worried."

"So sorry," he said, as he slipped his satchel off his shoulder. "Father found me in town and it was all rather awkward. I just couldn't seem to get away and then he asked me to help at the church. It's all been such a bother. I came as soon as I could. I'm so sorry."

He wiped the perspiration from his forehead and eyed the remaining sandwiches on the kitchen table.

"Tea's tepid but I'll put on the kettle," said Vera. "Sit down and let's have a look at the money!"

"The secretary said you were really talented," said Humphrey as he threw open the satchel and felt for the envelope. "I could tell she was very impressed."

"Well, he *is* talented," said Vera, putting her arm around James's waist. "And this is such an exciting moment!"

Humphrey's brows knit as he searched for the envelope. He pulled out all his books and flipped through the pages, holding them by their spines and shaking them. In fact, all of them looked fairly stunned, as Humphrey turned the linings of his pockets inside out one at a time.

"It's *gone* . . ." he said. "How could it be gone?"

They stared at each other.

Vera grabbed the satchel and went through it herself. She untied the pockets in the front and felt inside them. "Was it loose? Was it in an envelope?"

James joined her panic. "Is there some other place? Could you have stashed it some other place?"

Humphrey's lower lip quivered as he looked away from Mary and stared instead at the wooden floor. But there were no answers in the swirling wood grain, only a place for his tears to fall. Mary knew the guilt he felt and the hopelessness they all shared.

"Think," said James, with an edge to his voice. "Tell us exactly what you did after picking up the envelope."

"Remember Father asked you to get flour?" Mary prompted.

Humphrey stilled himself. "Yes, and I did," he began. "There was a queue and it was very frustrating. When I started back to the bench where Father had been, I was horrified that he wasn't there, because I'd left my satchel underneath the bench where Father was sitting. But it *was* there, untouched!" He stared down. "Then Father came back and said he'd gone to the post office for a telegram or something—church business, he said."

Mary sat on a chair, tired now from her chores. "And then?"

"Then I was even more frustrated because Father insisted I come with him to the church to repair a tree limb, of all the stupid things."

James lowered Hester to the floor. "A tree limb?"

"Yes," said Humphrey. "I simply couldn't believe it! But he insisted. He said it was dead, and a storm was coming and it might go through the window in a wind."

"So you went to the church," said Vera.

"Yes," said Humphrey.

"And you had the satchel with you then?" asked James.

"Absolutely, I did," said Humphrey. "I remember hanging it on a hook in the entranceway."

"By the door?" asked Mary.

Humphrey nodded. "Then we set about getting the limb off the tree."

"Just the two of you?" asked James.

"Yes," said Humphrey. "I fetched the tools from the shed—the rope, the saw, the axe—and then Father and I sawed off the branch and cut it up for firewood, and he even made me stack it." Humphrey began to cry. "I *told* him that I was in a hurry. I *said* that I had to get to your house. I didn't want to say why. I knew that you wanted it kept a secret."

"And the satchel was still on the hook when you'd finished?" asked Vera.

"Exactly where I'd left it," said Humphrey. "I was so careful to keep an eye on it, you know, because even the secretary was most uncomfortable giving me such a sum in cash."

At this point, Vera was beside herself. "Oh, James, what *can* we do?"

"I'll find it!" Humphrey said as he headed for the door. "I'll retrace my steps until I find it."

"I'll go with you!" said Mary, as she swung her sweater over her shoulder and closed the door behind them

Though they retraced Humphrey's steps to the church, the general store, the schoolhouse, post office, and through the woods, they could not find the envelope. Before he reached the cottage, he sat on a stump and sobbed inconsolably.

Mary put her arm around his shoulder. "Don't cry."

"How could I have been entrusted with such a sum of money and lose it?" He wiped his tears with his arm. "Surely I must be dreaming. I've run it over and over in my head these last hours and I can only imagine that the money must have been stolen from the satchel when it was under the bench." He ran his hands through his hair, pulling at the ends as if in punishment. "I didn't know Father was going to leave. He said he was resting!"

"How could you know?" Mary knelt in front of her brother. She tried to look at his face, but his body was doubled over and his head well down and hidden. "I've been thinking on it myself, and it's entirely possible that half the town knew of James's good fortune." She tried to sound as rational as possible. "Once I overheard some women talking at the store and one of them clearly called Mrs. Dryvens a gossip. What if she told people that James would be paid *cash*?" Her voice urged Humphrey to meet her gaze. "That's just the kind of thing that people would talk about, wouldn't they?"

Humphrey and Mary returned to the cottage.

"I'm sure it'll turn up," comforted Vera. "If someone pinched it, they'll not live with their conscience. It'll get the better of them."

She put a cup of strong tea in front of Humphrey. "Drink it," she said softly.

Humphrey slumped over the steaming cup. His eyes were red-rimmed and distant. Mary watched as he took a clumsy sip, but his hand was unsteady and he appeared to have difficulty swallowing. Finally, Humphrey cupped his face in his hands and the room grew still. Mary felt wretched and put her slim arm around his shoulder.

Chapter Twenty

Mary thought Vera was a natural mother. Having watched their own mother caring for Rachael and Eleanor, the older siblings had learned much about mothering. Vera was tender and loving, always smoothing Hester's pudgy arm or ankle, kissing her downy head at every opportunity. She relished each stage and wished it not to end. Each visit to the cottage began with the latest of Hester's developmental milestones—the discovery of her toes, pointing at something to get it, putting a spoon in her mouth.

James, too, was a devoted father, seemingly content to settle into the domestic security that had eluded him in his childhood. Mary was delighted to find him utterly devoted to both Vera and Hester. He loved his daughter with open and abiding affection, reveling in her babyhood with gentle, smiling eyes. Since the afternoon that the money went missing, Mary didn't hear James speak of it again. For a few weeks, he was quieter than usual, slightly depressed and slow in his work. But his even nature returned and he began to paint again, sharing his paints and brushes with anyone who kept his company. Mary wondered whether he'd accepted it so easily, as he had been forced to accept the many disappointments in his own life.

At Christmas, the family convened as usual at the Mills house. James surprised Vera with a delightful portrait of Hester, sitting on the front porch of their cottage with a beret on her head.

"Thank you," said Vera. "It's a perfect likeness! And I love that darling sweater she's wearing." Then she handed a present to James.

He pulled the paper off and turned the book right way round. "*Leaves of Grass* by Walt Whitman . . ." he read. "Thank you, Vera."

She smiled. "I found it at the thrift."

Father looked over the top of his glasses. "An American?"

Vera laughed. "A poet."

Everyone smiled except Father.

"I can't believe Hester's a whole year!" said Rachael as she took her by the hands, coaxing her to walk. "Come on! Come on!" she encouraged.

"I can't believe you're seven!" said Vera. "You're almost a lady!"

Rachael beamed with the thrill of being noticed.

Soon they assembled for Christmas dinner, which Mother, Mary, and Vera had worked for days to prepare. As always, when they were seated and after grace had been said, there was a toast to the King.

"The King!" boomed Father, as he raised his glass. "And absent friends," he added.

Mary, almost sixteen, felt most important as she worked alongside Vera and Mother. In the past year, she'd assumed a lot of new responsibilities and therefore had a wider knowledge of food. It was part of her domain now. She felt a sense of pride as Father remarked on how wonderful the food looked and how delicious it all tasted. It seemed they had absolutely everything they could possibly want for Christmas, even so far from England.

The dogs barked outside and Humphrey went to the door and let them in. Isobel was as big as Nell now, though not as wide. Humphrey put them on their blanket by the wall and gave the command to stay. Twice he had to return Isobel, who much preferred the carpet beside the fire.

"It's Christmas," said Mary. "Couldn't the dogs lie by the fire?"

Father looked over his glasses at his daughter. "Makes dogs soft."

When everyone had finished eating, and Vera got up to clear the table, she had an unmistakable limp.

"Whatever's happened?" asked Mother.

"It doesn't hurt," said Vera, as she continued to stack the dishes beside the sink.

But over the course of the evening, the limp was still notice-able so Mother insisted on examining the leg.

"Your knee is as swollen as a croquet ball!" Mother ran her hands lightly over the swelling. "Whatever did you do to it?"

"Nothing, Mother," said Vera again. She rolled her stock-ings back up and slid on her shoes. "It's time I got Hester off to bed. If it's still swollen in the morning, I'll see Dr. Cathcart."

Chapter Twenty-One

Humphrey fetched Dr. Cathcart the next morning.

"It's all the preparations for Christmas," Vera said to Mother who was washing the last of their breakfast dishes.

Mary sat on the floor with Hester. She'd stacked a tower of blocks for the baby to knock down, which she did just as Humphrey and Dr. Cathcart arrived. James and Humphrey waited with the baby while the women disappeared into the bedroom with the doctor.

Mary watched the young doctor tap on Vera's chest, front and back. After listening to her chest, looking in her throat and examining her eyes, Dr. Cathcart finally spoke.

"I'd suggest she see the specialist at the Kootenay Lake Hospital." He folded his stethoscope and stored it back in his black bag. "As a precaution."

"Obviously I need to stay here and tend to Eleanor and Hester," instructed Mother. "And James won't be allowed in the women's ward." She turned to Mary. "I think you should make the journey with your sister."

Within the hour, they were ready to leave. Reluctantly, James let go his wife's hand.

The main road was full of stumps sticking up under the snow and making it hard to go at any speed. The horse plodded along while Mary clasped Vera's hand, stroking it with her thumb.

"It'll be all right, Vere," she said. "Don't worry."

Vera's eyes were closed. Mary felt her own stomach churn. She chanted to the rhythm of the wheels' rotations—*she will be well . . . she will be well . . . she will be well . . .*

By the time they reached the hospital, Mary's hands were frozen. The warm festive feeling they'd all shared only yesterday seemed a distant memory.

The attendants put Vera in a wheelchair and whisked her inside, while Mary gathered her bags and hurried after the nurse who walked with an efficient gait down the shining linoleum hallway.

Mary felt panicked, trying to keep up, to keep in step with the nurse, to stay at her sister's side.

Vera was wheeled into a room with four beds, and was helped on to the bed nearest the window.

For a long time, Mary felt like a ghost, as no one acknowledged she was there. No one spoke to her or looked in her direction. Only Vera, who opened her eyes from time to time, noticed her.

The nurse was like a worker bee tending to the queen. Vera's clothes were gently removed and she was slid into a gown. The nurse placed a cloth on her forehead, a sick bowl at her side and a chart: Mrs. Vera Louise Constance Robinson. Age 18.

Then just when Mary thought she might faint from standing still for so long, the nurse turned to her with a kind, quiet voice and said, "You must be exhausted, dear. Sit in the chair, and tonight you can sleep in the bed beside your sister."

She bustled out and in within the same minute. "Don't worry, duckie," she said to Mary, "She's in good hands now."

But Mary spent a worrisome day, as various doctors and interns filtered in and out, studying charts and clipboards and Vera herself—a specimen, it seemed, behind a white curtain. Then night fell, and with it came fitful sleep, as she awoke to the queer sounds of hospital regimen. Often, Mary swung out of bed and sat in the chair beside Vera, holding the cloth on her forehead, then rinsing it in the bowl of cool water and reapplying it. Or she'd watch the night nurse do the same.

The room was dimly lit and Mary was relieved when the blackness beyond the window faded into the purple mountain in the distance. The fresh light of day revealed a paler looking Vera, dark circles under her eyes. The nurse and doctor entered the room and asked Mary to wait in the hallway.

She leaned against the wall as she waited and wondered. Then the door opened and the doctor appeared looking very grave.

"I have some rather bad news," he began, looking sympathetically at Mary. "Your sister has TB."

"TB?" asked Mary.

"Tuberculosis," clarified the doctor. "But we do seem to have caught this very early on and I . . ."

At the very moment when Mary thought she might burst open with dread, James and Father strode down the hallway toward them.

"You're her husband?" asked the doctor.

"I am," answered James, "and this is Vera's father, Reverend Rudyard Mills."

"I'm afraid it's TB," he said, as he reached a comforting hand to James's arm. "But we've got it very early on and as is often the case with children and young people, it's in her joints. It's not yet pulmonary. So we're hoping the outlook to be favorable."

Mary stared at the doctor, wondering whether he might have made a mistake. Could you possibly be talking about another Vera? Did he have the test results mixed up?

The doctor cleared his throat. "She'll need a separate room in the house, with a balcony if possible," he said. "Her own lavatory and a nurse, of course. Minimal disruptions. Rest and routine ministrations will see her through."

Father's face turned white. It was evident that the words didn't come easily. "We haven't the money." He stared at the floor.

Mary knew that the doctor had presumed the family was well off. Father's fine English clothes and his upper class accent, relics from a past that seemed desperately far away, had fooled the doctor.

There was an uncomfortable silence. "Then she's to go directly to the sanatorium."

James looked puzzled. "Sanatorium?"

"The Valleyview sanatorium," began the doctor. "West of Kamloops, on the lakeshore. Beautiful location and lovely warm air. Top notch care. Don't fret."

"I'll care for her at home," offered James.

"But the baby?" asked Mary.

"The disease is contagious and the baby would be susceptible." The doctor read the pain on James's face. "In time, perhaps. But first Vera will need treatment. Valleyview is the best in the area, newly built, elevated, sunny and dry. When she's stronger, she may have visitors. For two dollars a night, I believe family members are welcome in the administrative building. The rail line passes through there now, and Nurse Wheelright will accompany Vera and settle her in." He looked at their numb expressions. "The nurses are *very* capable at Valleyview."

Tears slid down Mary's face.

"There, now," said the doctor. "Why don't you pack up your sister's things? Unfortunately, the clothing she arrived in is likely contaminated and will be burned, but you may take her combs and whatnot from her bedside table. Valleyview will provide gowns, sheets, towels, and slippers." The doctor pulled a clean handkerchief from his coat pocket and handed it to Mary.

James, Mary, and Father stepped quietly into Vera's room. She slept, with her face turned toward the window. No one knew how to proceed. Mary felt that if a comforting hand fell onto her shoulder, her body would shatter like broken glass. Mary watched Father move softly toward the bed.

Vera's dress and stockings had already been cleared away, but whoever did so had emptied the pockets onto the bedside table. Father took them one by one into his hand—the brooch with Hester's photograph, her everyday combs, and finally, the whistle he had given her for Nell.

"Oh God," he whispered. "Above all evil and above all good, help us now." He closed his eyes and clasped the whistle to his chest.

Father walked into the hallway, James followed, and the older man dropped Vera's personal items into his hands. No words were exchanged.

Then Rudyard Mills did a strange thing. Before James closed his hand on the items, the old man retrieved the whistle. Mary watched him now put the whistle to his lips and blow into it, ever so softly, mostly air without much sound, a call without the urgency to come. He handed it back to James.

"It still works," said Father without looking up. "Though I know she never uses it."

Mary felt herself growing weak in the knees and closed her eyes. A fury of blood coursed now through her body and she welcomed the warmth and sensation.

Mary opened her eyes and shone her flashlight on Grandad.

He was sitting on the bottom step with his leg stretched straight and his crutches on the stones beside him. "Are you all right?" His mustache turned down in worry.

Mary's eyes fixed on his face. "I feel a little tired. I feel that I've . . ."

Grandad knit his brow and looked at her as though she might be ill. "You seem a touch dazed, dear."

She stared at him still, deep into his blue eyes, Humphrey's blue eyes. She'd been back to Bircher and she'd been in Mary's consciousness again. The trick. The journey. Whatever it was had happened again and this time it had been *desperately* sad. Her Grandad had suffered. And Vera. *Good God!* Vera had tuberculosis and would be sent away! Hester would be without her mother . . . Mary felt deep heartache as she looked at Grandad and remembered it all.

He reached for her hand. "Perhaps we better go back."

"Oh, Grandad, I've *been* back! And it's all so sad . . ." Mary felt overwhelmed to bursting.

Grandad looked at her quizzically. "I think you're overreacting. Taking the traps will make a dent in his activities. He won't want to keep buying them every time they disappear."

Mary had brought the events of the past forward in time and had confused them, confused Grandad. She needed to still herself for what was happening at this moment.

"Wait here," she said, dully. "There's one more." Mary disappeared into the darkness to retrieve the other trap.

Her legs ached and her head was heavy, but she was back in this world and that felt good in some respects. There were stones beneath her feet, rocks rubbing against each other as she walked over them toward the remaining trap. There had been too much to handle in Bircher, a place that now felt as familiar as her pockets. It felt good to be back in her world, where Grandad was not a boy, but a mischievous old man, sitting like an injured duck on the salty beach. *The Empire is at war!* That's what Humphrey had shouted through the screen door in 1914—almost seventy-years ago. Mary's heart stalled, then raced as the two worlds bumped about in her brain.

She returned with the trap and helped Grandad up the stairs. They stood in the garage where the traps were carefully stacked on top of the previous three.

Grandad leaned against his workbench for support. "Perhaps we could gather enough to fashion one large trap for Mr. Barry," he suggested. "We could bait it with cheap, liqueur-filled chocolates."

Aunt Hester stood in the doorway, her hands on her hips, wagging her finger at her uncle. "You're an *appalling* influence."

Mary didn't dare speak again, lest she confuse her worlds.

Chapter Twenty-Two

Grandad looked sheepish. "Sorry."

"You always say that and then you go ahead and do something mischievous," scolded Aunt Hester. "Is this what a grandfather with a broken leg does to get well?" She didn't wait for an answer, but turned and led them back to the house.

They were now sitting around the dining room table, eyes downcast.

"I'm not abandoning the mission," said Grandad in a quiet voice.

Hester opened a cookie tin and tipped it in Humphrey's direction.

"Have you thought about Mother?" said Aunt Hester, softening a little. "You know she'd love it down here." She scratched her forehead with her thumb. "The sea, the beach, the otters, the whole darn thing. I'd bet she'd spend the day just sitting in this chair, figuring out the tides and clouds, identifying the birds and shrubs."

Grandad reached down and patted Jester's head.

"And she'd love this absurd adventure of yours," Aunt Hester continued, with scarcely detectable approval. "I shouldn't even tell you this, but a few years ago, she set free the neighbor's mink. Can't domesticate wild things, she told me, and raising creatures for fashion was downright inhumane. So off she went at midnight, rubber boots on her feet and dressed all in black with a pair of wire clippers in her pocket. Then snip, snip, she cut a hole in the wire and watched as the poor things disappeared into the night."

"You're having us on," said Grandad. "What if she'd been caught?"

"You're one to talk," laughed Aunt Hester. "She figured no right-minded lawmaker would throw an old woman wearing gumboots in the slammer who was freeing creatures that shouldn't have been captive in the first place."

Mary beamed. "That's awesome!"

"Illegal," said Aunt Hester. "But there you go. That's Mother for you. Just like when I was small and she'd dote over our old dog Nell, and those treasured cows. Remember dear Miss Milk and Martha Tree Stump?"

Mary froze. She wanted to say *Yes! I do remember that!* But she willed herself to be silent, wanting more stories of Mary—the other Mary.

Grandad laughed. "Do you know that the moment the calf was born, she named her Martha. She insisted."

Hester smiled. "I didn't know it was Mother that named her."

"After her best friend in England." Grandad ran his hand over Jester's head. "Then your Aunt Rachael made an awful fuss and Mary felt sorry for her, and . . ."

"*Mary* named her Martha," Mary interjected.

Aunt Hester stared at Mary. "Yes, that's right."

Mary felt awash in confusion. Her mind raced to the day she and Mum arrived at the house and how they were looking at the photographs. Mum had told her that she was named after Mary, and that Mary was Hester's mother. But Mary now knew better. Running through the woods in the snow, her skirts hindering her progress, falling now and racing back to find Vera giving birth to a baby girl—Hester. It *was* Hester, so perfect and new. Mary saw *Vera* give birth, absolutely Vera, pushing the baby into the world with sweat and pain and exhaustion beyond anything she'd ever seen. It was Vera, *not* Mary. She was *there*.

"I thought . . ." Mary stopped herself.

Grandad patted the dog at his side. "You thought what?"

"I'm so confused about . . ." She stared down, escaping eye contact. "It's okay."

Grandad looked at Mary over his bifocals. "What is confusing?"

"What?" Mary stared at the fireplace. "Excuse me," she said, getting up and walking out to the front hall.

Mary's throat felt constricted; her heart was racing. She felt faint and sat on the hall chair. Grandad and Aunt Hester were still talking in the living room. Their voices were soft at first. Mary heard Hester, "For God's sake, Uncle Humphrey, it's all worked out. I had such a lovely childhood. A wonderful, memorable, loving childhood. I wanted for nothing. Nothing. I didn't even know my mother well enough to miss her. I knew only one mother who adored me, Mary."

Goose bumps sprang up on Mary's arms. Surely Vera didn't *die* of TB? Hadn't they caught it early? Mary's head was spinning. Then she heard Grandad crying.

"I would've given my life for hers," he sobbed. "She had a child."

"But you have Nora," said Aunt Hester, "And Mary and Kip. You can't wish to exchange one life for another."

After a time, there was quiet. When Mary returned to the living room, Aunt Hester sat alone at the table by the window.

"Your Grandad's gone to his den." Aunt Hester pulled out the game of *Spellicans*, opened the cardboard box and emptied the thin wooden sticks onto the table.

"You first," she said to Mary as she handed her the hooked stick.

"I'm not feeling too well," said Mary, putting down the hook.

Hester raised her eyebrows. "You're overtired, too. Is it your tummy?"

"A little."

"Go to bed, dear. I'll bring up a water bottle."

Mary leaned down and gave her aunt a hug.

"Snuggle up in bed and have sweet dreams."

"I'm not quite sure about my dreams these days," said Mary. "They're not so sweet."

Mary closed her bedroom door behind her. She stuffed her hands deep into her pockets and pulled out the whistle. It was hard enough trying to sort out the present, let alone the past.

The moment she held the whistle in her hand, a vivid image of Vera flashed in her mind. She was asleep in her hospital bed, newly diagnosed with tuberculosis. *No, this was too painful, too much.* Mary knew that if she blew the whistle, she would return to Bircher. She couldn't go back and see her sister die. She did not want any more of this drama. The whole thing was too confusing now, painful, impossibly sad. She couldn't *bear* to lose Vera. Yet no one spoke of her now. She must be dead! *No! I will not blow this whistle again.*

Yet while Mary willed herself to refrain from using this instrument of insight that she now held, squeezed in her hand, soft and warm—she was *drawn* to it. She fought with herself to never go back to Bircher. She knew enough. She would stop. She would get rid of the whistle. *Throw it out! Smash it!*

Mary opened the bathroom window and held the whistle tight in her palm. *You can't make me*, she thought. *You can't make me.* But even as she chanted these words in her head, the picture of Vera in her hospital bed sprang to mind and she slowly put the whistle to her lips.

Her eyes closed and she fought the vortex as it spun the feeling from her body yet again, whipping her against the whirlpool that brought her down. Willing herself not to descend, trying to grip edges that were permeable, she ceased to feel anything but her angry heart, struggling in her tired chest. She opened her eyes and saw Mary, Humphrey's sister, drawing nearer and nearer until they were united.

The room was warm now, and Mary felt conspicuously untidy as her clothes had been slept in and her hair was flyaway. There was a tea stain on her front, when she'd shakily taken her first sip at daybreak.

James and Father assisted the nurse as Vera was transferred to a wheelchair. Clearly overwhelmed by this sudden turn of events, Vera stared into Mary's eyes.

"Hester?" she whispered.

"I'll make sure Hester is happy," said Mary. "I'll make *sure* of it. You needn't worry about her. *Promise*." Mary crossed her heart with her fist.

And then Vera did cry, deep and desperate, into her hand. James pulled her head into his chest and stroked her hair while she wept, then settled her back into the chair. Father looked on, ashen-faced and forlorn.

"There're tests to be done, sir," said the nurse, "before she's off to Valleyview. Best we make a start."

"*Promise*," Mary whispered again before Vera disappeared down the hallway.

Chapter Twenty-Three

"How will I care for her?" James looked down at his sleeping child. "How can I work and care for her?"

Mary leaned forward in her chair. "We'll find a way," she said. "Between the lot of us."

Humphrey nodded, then leaned forward and stuffed a log into the stove.

Early evening had crept upon them; they were weary now from the day. Mary had retrieved Hester from Mother. The little girl had spent a blissful day with Rachael, Eleanor, and the boisterous dogs. Back in her own home, Hester had fallen easily asleep in the comforting arms of her father, who looked down at her now and wondered aloud what would become of them. Mary and Humphrey, feeling desperately sad themselves, tried to comfort their brother-in-law.

"But Vera does everything important," said James. "She bathes her and dresses her and makes the soup she likes."

"I'll help you," said Mary. "I can come every day and make the soup . . ." But Mary looked into James's eyes and saw only grief. "Let's get a fire roaring and we'll have a cup of tea."

Mary settled Hester on her bed, while Humphrey put the kettle to boil. They had a cup of tea before Hester woke. Mary scooped her up as Vera did and put her in the metal washtub filled with warm water and a cup to play with.

Hester poured and filled the cup while Mary took a clean cloth from the dresser drawer and washed her. James set about doing domestic chores, mechanically, quietly. Hester splashed her flat palms on the water's surface gleefully.

"Time to get you in a clean square." Mary carefully lifted Hester from the bath and held tight to her slippery skin while she patted her dry with a towel. She lay the baby down on the big bed, fastened on a fresh nappy, and dressed her warmly. She gently brushed the fine blonde curls on Hester's head and put her on the floor where she toddled off to her father.

"Mummy?" asked Hester.

James drew in his lips and worked hard not to cry.

Humphrey moved closer to James, though he couldn't find anything comforting to say. There was only one thing on his mind. "If only I hadn't lost the money," he began. "You might have afforded private care." His chin fell to his chest.

These words seemed to shatter James further, for the reminder that the money was gone, and that Humphrey still suffered from the loss.

"You mustn't say that," James replied. "We might have already spent that money on a studio or something else." He was quiet for a moment. "In any case, the doctor said the sanatorium was top notch, the best in Canada. We should be thankful it's nearby."

Mary was grateful for his optimism.

There were footsteps, and Father appeared in the doorway. "Mary and Humphrey, it's time to come home." The old man didn't enter the room.

Humphrey stood and Mary slipped onto the front porch and closed the door behind her.

"He's feeling rather sad," Mary whispered, as she gently held the door closed. "He's afraid he'll lose Vera."

"Aren't we *all*?" asked Father, as he massaged his knuckles on one hand.

Mary's emotions got the better of her again as tears slid from her eyes. "Yes," she sniffed, "but James is Vera's husband!"

"Because of the baby."

For the first time, Mary's father appeared to her as a dark character, a man with a crippled heart. "*No*, Father," whispered Mary, pleading for understanding. "They *love* each other. He's afraid. He doesn't think he can care for the baby and work at the same time." Mary felt incredulous that her father, whose job it was to comfort and counsel, could be so insensitive. She felt as though she was the parent and he was the child.

"Life goes on," said Father. "We must all pray for Vera." And then he was gone.

Mary managed to get James near the warmth of the fire in a chair where he took another cup of tea and a biscuit. She put Hester in his lap with some warm milk. Then Mary and Humphrey pulled on their coats and stood by the door.

"You'll be *just* fine," Mary encouraged. "We'll all get through this together. You'll see."

Humphrey nodded, though he was again at a loss for words. James nodded and tried a smile.

Mary thought he looked much improved, and, as she backed out the door, she talked herself into believing that James would be all right, that Hester would be fine, that Vera would survive.

"Good girl," she said to Nell as she patted the dog's head, then closed the door and started through the snow. Humphrey walked behind her, and there was only the sound of footsteps and sniffling noses.

"I'm just going to look in on the cows," said Mary as they neared the barn. "I'll see you in the house."

Mary threw herself down on the straw and sobbed until her grief and fear had eased to a bearable level.

She looked up at Martha Tree Trunk staring at her. The chickens, plump on their roosts, quizzically cocked their dotty heads in her direction. Mary walked to the house, gave her mother a hug and tied a clean apron around her waist.

After dinner, Mary pushed aside her plate and rested her head on her folded arms.

"Go to bed," said Mother. "You're exhausted."

As Mary climbed the stairs, she heard Mother ask Humphrey to deliver some dinner to James and Hester.

"Take Isobel and come right home," said Father. "It's dark."

Humphrey buttoned his coat and disappeared into the darkness with the dog, but returned unexpectedly soon with the news that James was not faring well.

Mary raced down the stairs. "I have to go!" she said.

"I'll go!" Father returned.

At once, the entire family, save Eleanor, had the same thought—Father would be the worst possible candidate to handle James.

"Hester might want me." Mary looked pleadingly at her father, hoping he'd understand the urgency she now felt, praying she wouldn't have to assert herself any further. "I *promised* Vera."

"What the devil are you on about, child?" roared Father. "Vera has a husband. Isn't he capable of caring for his own child?"

Mother stood in the doorway with Eleanor at her side. "Rudyard," she began, summoning her strength, "we're going to have to invite James and Hester here. He can't possibly manage alone with her, trying to earn a wage and care for her properly. He'll need good food and moral support. Any man would. And the baby will be distracted by the girl's attentions, she'll miss her mother less over here. You know that."

Rudyard Mills looked at his wife without expression. She was right, of course. There could be no denying entrance to his grandchild. And he couldn't have the child without the father. The old man grimaced and pulled at the end of his beard.

Mother buttoned her coat and laced her boots. "Hester'll sleep with Mary and Rachael, James'll have a cot beside Humphrey. I'll be back as soon as I can." She tied a scarf beneath her chin and began to lace her boots.

Mary looked pained at this sudden turn of events. Though she was happy of James and Hester's company, she knew how Father felt about James.

Mother and Mary walked briskly through the woods with a lamp. Isobel bounded ahead of them. As they neared the cabin, Mary saw Hester standing on the porch in stocking feet. Tears streamed down her cheeks.

"Goodness me!" said Mother. "Let's get you inside."

Mother took Hester inside and found James in much the same mournful state. "It's all right," she whispered in Hester's ear, as she smoothed circles around and around the little girl's small back. "Everything's all right." Hester's lower lip quivered.

Mary felt a terrible anger rise up inside her. She turned and glared at James. "I promised Vera that I'd take care of Hester," she began. "But I'm not going to do it alone. *Do you hear me?*"

"Mary!" Mother looked aghast.

"We all feel dreadful. You're not the only one. You can't just sit there staring stupidly, letting Hester wander about!"

James sat silently, incredulous.

"You can't ignore her like she was one of the dogs."

"Good *gracious*, girl!" said Mother. "What in the devil has got into you?" She rose and walked to where James now stood. Mother took his arm at his elbow and directed him toward the bedroom. "Let's pack your things now."

After a time, Mother emerged with James, carrying Hester and a small carpet bag. He pulled on his woolen coat and found Hester her hat and mittens. When at last they seemed ready to proceed home, James went back to the bedroom for a book and slipped it into his coat pocket.

Mary felt ashamed. She should *not* have lost her temper, especially in front of Hester. Her lower lip trembled and she felt sweaty and overwhelmed. Uneasily waiting by the door, she buttoned her coat and tied a scarf over her head. She was a picture of distress, as feelings of frustration, anger and upset raged in her body.

With Hester in his arms now, James walked out the door, avoiding Mary's gaze.

The four of them trudged through the path toward home. Hester's small arms were wrapped around her father's neck.

Chapter Twenty-Four

If the Mills house hadn't been cozy before, it certainly was now. Eight people beneath one small roof felt a squeeze. The children loved having their brother-in-law and niece in residence. Hester was steady entertainment for Eleanor and Rachael, who followed her about, giggling and guiding her in safe directions.

James was quiet and helpful. He clearly worked at keeping occupied, staying on the brink of exhaustion so sleep would come fast and deep. He couldn't bear to contemplate Vera's condition more than was necessary. He was enduring the days until her return and working double time to earn money for nursing care.

Rudyard Mills, on the other hand, was becoming cross more often, stubbornly taking long walks with the dogs in place of proper meals. He grew gaunt, more stooped, inclined not to sleep well and so falling fast asleep in his old chair by the fire. Mother would slip the pipe from his hand while he slept and cover him with a blanket. Isobel, aware that her master slept, nibbled at the fabric of the old chair. The little girls, consumed by their world of play and pretend, didn't notice the change in him. Mary and Humphrey, on the other hand, were aware of their father's declining health.

Finally, Mother asked Dr. Cathcart around to examine Father, as he'd cancelled two sermons and had taken to his bed for three consecutive days. Although Dr. Cathcart could not find any conclusive diagnosis, he suggested to Mother that Father was weakened by the cold climate and difficult times.

"Perhaps you should think of moving to the coast," he suggested, "where the climate is mild, and the lifestyle more like that of England." He glanced out the window at the steep drifts of snow. "I hear Victoria is quite civilized."

During this time of duress, Mary anticipated the evening's quiet to write Vera. With the company of the oil lamp's soft glow and the gentle breathing of the girls in the big bed, Mary dipped her pen in ink and began.

May, 1915

Dear Vera,

The snow and ice of winter have finally melted into spring, a great relief as we needn't worry about the pipes freezing anymore. Hester is happy not to be bundled so warmly as she detests the scratchy beret Aunt Alice sent from England. She's a picture of you now, with her blonde curls lengthening and sitting on her shoulders.

I don't want you to worry about Hester. You must concentrate on getting well. James is clearing land for the farmers in the mornings and painting in the afternoon. He plays with Hester and the girls while Mother and I get the dinner on and the washing done. Hester, Rachael, and

I sleep together upstairs. She's just a little version of you, lying beside me! It's so very strange.

As I've said before, we talk of you often, of how you are getting stronger and better and will come home soon. So you mustn't make us into liars. Hester says "Mummy" often and she calls me "Tee Mawee." She calls food "um" and she calls James, "Daddy." She's so very dear.

As you know, Mother and Father are selling the land here and moving to Victoria. As promised, I'll stay on with James and care for Hester. The three of us will move back to the cottage when Mother and Father journey to Victoria with the children. Aunt Barbara will care for the little girls so Mother may prepare the house for whomever buys it, and Father can say a proper goodbye to his parishioners.

I'm more than pleased to be staying here in Bircher as I don't fancy sharing Auntie's rather small house with so many. Further, I'm just as happy to leave my studies for the time being, as it's rumored that a rather wicked school-teacher will replace Miss Beedy in the fall.

Poor Miss Beedy's brother was hit with shrapnel in the trenches. She's returning to her family home in England. Reading, I think.

And remember the Browns who lived near Grandmama? Well, poor Mr. Brown lost his wife and two children aboard the Lusitania. I heard it first in the village and later read it in one of Mr. Wilks' copies of the Illustrated London News. Luckily, the three youngest children were at home with the nurse.

Enclosed is a pair of slippers I've knitted for you. Mrs. Fairclough very kindly gave me the leftover wool from a sweater she knitted for Hester. And wouldn't you know, she *always gives us a bit of sugar from her own rations. Despite the very long, cold winter, our dear neighbors warm my heart with their continued generosity.*

> *Your devoted sister,*
> *Mary*

One day, Mother announced that the search was on for a nurse.

"A *nurse?*" asked Mary. "Whatever for?"

"Hester, of course. James isn't about to move to Victoria, so he'll need some help until Vera comes home. Father figures there're plenty of young women whose husbands are overseas. James could do the man's work in exchange for some house-keeping and so on."

"That doesn't sound a bad plan," said James who watched Hester stuff her paisley cat in a tea tin and close the lid.

Mary felt as if plans were made without consulting her first. "But I *promised* Vera, Mother. I crossed my heart that *I* would take care of Hester. Not some other woman she doesn't even know, any old woman who might be beastly to Hester if she was naughty." Mary's lip started to tremble. "I can't leave Bircher. I *won't* leave Hester. That's final."

Mother put her arm around Mary sympathetically. "Dear, I know how you feel, and believe me, I have those feelings myself. Remember, I'm Hester's Granny . . . but if we move to town, we have so many more opportunities open to us. We'll live with Aunt Barbara and Uncle Angus until we can afford a flat. The schooling is better. Most importantly, we may have the opportunity to afford private care for Vera as soon as we're settled on our own somewhere."

"Are you mad?" asked Mary, her eyes welling with tears. "Vera will want to come here, to Bircher, where she'll be with James and Hester."

"Oh, Mary," said Mother and she took her in her arms for a long time. "Darling Mary."

Mary pulled away. "I'm staying here, Mother." Mary could hardly believe she said it. But she had, and she'd meant it.

"Mary," James began.

"I promised Vera," Mary repeated. "I promised she shouldn't worry about Hester."

"Your father won't allow it. Imagine what people will say, dear. You have to at least think about that!"

"He can't stop me from doing the right thing. I don't care what other people say. And why should he? He's leaving this place."

Mother took Mary's hands as she'd done on the day Vera was married. She bit her lip. "Vera's illness gives Father an excuse to leave Bircher. You know he's never *really* wanted to come to Canada. He doesn't see this as home. He's been extremely agitated since leaving England."

"Then why did we come to this bloody awful place?" Mary bellowed, her chin trembling.

"Mary!"

"Excuse me, Mother, but sometimes I don't understand why we had to leave Beddington at all . . . why we had to sell all of our wonderful things just to make a dreadful voyage here to this lonely place! I *miss* the animals and I *miss* Grandmama."

"Mary, it's entirely understandable that yet another move is somewhat daunting."

"*Daunting*, Mother! I wouldn't move to the tropics if I were given passage. I *promised* Vera that Hester would be *my charge*. I promised." Mary crossed her arms. "I've just written Vera, Mother, and I've told her that I'm staying in Bircher."

Mother cleared her throat. "Uncle Angus's school is doing rather well and he tells Father that the town is more like England than England! Imagine! It might be just the thing to lift his spirits, to stop what I believe to be a dreadful homesickness. And you've certainly a touch of it, too. Not to mention a bloody great dose of bad temper."

Mary stared at her mother and said one last time, "I promised."

Chapter Twenty-Five

June, 1915

Dear Mary,

As you know, Mother, Father, Eleanor, Rachael and Humphrey came yesterday to see me, but all I could do was stand on the verandah while they stood on the lawns and waved. You were quite right not to come, as I don't think I could bear to see my darling Hester and not hold her and love her. I can't believe how big Eleanor and Rachael have grown. It seems I've missed so much.

Mother wrote that the house has finally sold to an Irishman, but it will be some time before he arrives. Father's spirits have lifted somewhat, though he's still not the father we knew in England. Even his letters seem peculiarly formal. I imagine it's the strain of it all. At least he can focus his attentions on his new position in Victoria.

I do hope he's leaving Bircher because it's his decision and not because of my ill health. He seems set on having me transported to Victoria almost as soon as they find lodging with a separate room for the nurse. I've hardly the heart to write Mother that I don't want to go to Victoria. I've no intention of living in town, no matter how much it seems like England. I've come to adore this country, I really have.

Humphrey tells me there are more motorcars in town, all very noisy and unreliable. The sanatorium has a Ford. I wrote Humphrey and told him to come and see it very soon, but he didn't mention it in his letter. In fact, it was the shortest letter I've had, and really quite dull. Is Humphrey very sad about moving to Victoria?

I've met a friend here called Mary-Anne and she and I find some happiness talking about the families we miss so very much. She was as ill as I and is now on the mend. Her family came to visit and I was able to see them on the lawn, too. Her mother seemed a perfect friend for ours. Although they didn't visit at the same time, we're conspiring to have them meet. We laugh and cry about these absurd visits. I share Mother's biscuits with her, and she shares a lemon cake her mother always brings. It's inevitably stale, as it's traveled so far, but we don't care. It's something from a real home.

We're not supposed to discuss our illnesses, but Mary-Anne and I make all sorts of jokes about the pulse and temperature taking which gets very tedious. They expect us to take light exercise on the grounds where there are an alarming number of rattlesnakes!

There's regular train service here now, so I'm hoping that soon the matron will allow all of you to see me again soon, when it's time. The Chinese laundryman makes a white mouse out of a table napkin and cleverly has it jumping along his forearm! I know that Hester would love it. I'll get him to teach me how to do it.

I'm indebted to you for all you've done for me. How can I ever repay you? I'll think of something.

Your loving sister,

Vera

P.S. Sometimes I see soldiers arriving by ambulance. Poor things. You can't imagine what they've suffered, with pulmonary tuberculosis on top of it all! I'm really rather lucky.

July 15, 1915

Dear Vera,

James has been planting and irrigating today and came home exhausted but still wanting to paint. It seems that Victoria's town hall has commissioned two paintings for the reception. One of the mountains to the south and one of a rather picturesque farmhouse! He feels quite cheered to have finally made another sale. An artist makes such a beastly living.

Hester is recovering from a cold that really hasn't bothered her much except in the evening. I took her into bed with me and gave her a hot water bottle. Dr. Cathcart called this morning. He said for her to get lots of rest and to bed early. I'm happy of that!

As you know, Mother, Father, Humphrey, and the girls have traveled to Victoria for a fortnight. Father is going to discuss his employment with Uncle Angus and the children will become acquainted with their cousins. Humphrey has been working at odd jobs that need doing before the start of term. I miss him very much. Aunt Barbara has a used carpet sweeper for Mother that she's rather excited about. She's going to leave the girls with Aunt Barbara so she can set to work getting the house prepared for the Irishman.

Miss Milk and Martha Tree Trunk are happily living in their new shelter that James, Mr. Wilks, and Humphrey built. Hester loves to watch the milking, especially when James sprays the milk at Nell who tries to lick it off her whiskers before it drips to the floor!

There will be much packing and preparing the house for the Irishman and his family. We've heard there are eight children!

I've met a girl my age called Ethel Parker. Of course, she doesn't have a baby to care for as I do, but she is often responsible for her young brother of four, Walter, who is darling and plays rather well with Hester. We go to the lakeside together and take the children in the water and splash about. She and I have wonderful times together. I'm so thankful for her company.

Dear Vera, you must know that James adores you thoroughly and that he waits for your return. Don't think for a minute that you've caused any upset. Father has never seemed himself since just before we left England. In fact, when I think back on our last days at Beddington, he was dreadfully bad-tempered. Do you remember? And don't fret about Humphrey. He'll be himself as soon as you are well.

You are always in our thoughts and prayers,
Your loving sister,
Mary

September 5, 1915

Dear Mary,

I'm sorry I haven't written for so long, but I had a set-back and became ill and really rather depressed, and I often wondered if I would see my dear Hester and the family ever again. But I feel better now and have been out in the garden with Mary-Anne, gossiping about all the inmates. She's fallen asleep, which means a good opportunity to write.

Do you think Hester will know who I am? Will she remember me? Mother brought in some embroidery and I've made her a lovely little pillow with flowers on a plum background.

I've been so very lucky that you've taken her under your wing. Mary-Anne told me that in Paris when babies are born to mothers with TB, they are often taken away and raised by peasant families in the country. I can't imagine it!

I met a man here who lost his leg in the war. He was afraid to write and tell his wife about it for fear that she'd reject him! The poor man was terribly distraught. But I helped him write the letter and then he received one in return and of course, it was full of love and understanding. I wouldn't think much of his wife if she couldn't understand his dreadful circumstances. On top of all this, he's got a terrible cough and must remain in bed for a very long time.

Some people's lives are so odd. Then again, I suppose most of the people in Bircher think us entirely odd. James and I have corresponded about possibly moving from Bircher, maybe to the coast where James might work in the lumberyards, or on a fishing boat. Really, I think what we need is a fresh start in a new place.

I must go. They're calling us for tea. You should see the beastly nurse who dispenses sugar! Mary Anne and I suspect her a German spy!

Pray that I can come home soon. I'm so terribly homesick.
All my love,
Vera

Mary re-read the letter, then brought herself back to the moment, back to Hester who was emptying the pots from the cupboard. A busy little girl, almost two now, Hester was active and interested in the world. Mary didn't dare let on in her letters how taxing these days had been for her with the rest of the family in Victoria. How desperate she'd felt so often, how lonely she was, how patient she needed to be with Hester but how hard it was to have patience all the time.

She longed to be in her old bed with Vera and Rachael. Instead, she found herself installed in Vera's bedroom, sharing the double bed with Hester while James slept on a cot by the fire.

"Let's put these away now," said Mary. And as she loaded the pots back into the cupboard, Hester streaked out the door and down the stairs.

"Wait!" called Mary, who abandoned the half-churned butter in the kitchen.

She caught up to Hester but couldn't get a hold on the day. When she woke in the morning, James had already gone to pick fruit. Hester woke early, as usual, out of sorts and unable to be happy for a minute. She'd thrown her porridge on the floor in a temper and pulled Nell's tail. Then when Mary was dressing, she'd got into her hairpins and pulled them all apart.

Now she was careening down the path to the barn, with no shoes on and the weather far and away into autumn. Mary hadn't eaten breakfast and desperately needed to go to the bathroom, but it looked like another day of racing after this tornado who was by now trying to work her way through the split rail fence.

On the other side of the fencing, Mary saw Ethel Rogers racing toward her, and, as she neared, she saw tears streaming down her friend's face.

Mary scooped Hester in her arms and walked as fast as she could toward Ethel. "Whatever's the matter?" she asked as she put a comforting arm about her friend's back. "Poor Ethel, what is it?"

Ethel gathered herself together. "Mother says I'm not to be friends with you anymore because of the way you're living." She stared down at the ground.

Mary looked incredulous and removed her hand from Ethel's back. "But I can't *help* it!" she said. "I *must* live this way! I'm looking after my sister's child!"

"*I* understand it all," said Ethel, dabbing at her tears, "but Mother and Father say people talk and well . . . there's been talk about you living with James while Vera's away . . ."

"Vera's not *away!* She's *sick!*" Mary put Hester down. "And I'm James's *sister-in-law!* I'm Hester's *aunt!* I made a promise to my sister that I would look after Hester. I *promised!* The whole family's moving to Victoria! I can't leave James alone with her!"

"I'm sorry," said Ethel. "But I must be off. Mother took Walter to Mrs. Saymer's and this was my only chance to explain it all. I just didn't want you to think I wasn't your friend anymore. I'm so, *so* sorry, I'll miss you and Hester and I know that Walter will, too. I wish so much that we could still be friends. Perhaps when we're grown . . ."

Ethel gave Mary a quick hug, then turned and ran away.

"If you understand it!" yelled Mary, "why can't you do the right thing? Why can't *anyone* do the right thing?"

Ethel stopped and stared back at Mary, then turned and kept running even as Mary yelled, "*Why is everyone so beastly?*" By this time, Mary was hoarse from yelling and spiraling into a rage. The unfairness in the world was swallowing her hopes and happiness.

Mary's governess had always told her that life was not fair. But only now did she deeply feel the meaning of it, feel the sorrow of unfolding events that were not of her making. She felt in her heart that she was doing the right thing, yet she received so much condemnation. And what would be the consequences of Mary not caring for Hester? Wouldn't that be immeasurably worse?

She scooped up Hester and turned in the opposite direction, crying as she ran, the baby bouncing on her hip. She reached the house and let Hester down on the porch. Nell was not there. The door was wide open.

"Nell!" yelled Mary with a cathartic bellow. "Nell!"

The volume of her aunt's voice caused Hester to stare. She looked up with bright eyes, so innocent of all that happened around her. She wasn't to blame. Mary's lower lip quivered as she fought back tears.

"You're a lamb," she said to Hester. Mary reached into her pocket and pulled from it the whistle.

"Watch, Hester," said Mary. "Nell will come out of the forest before you can say 'All the King's Horses'."

Then Mary blew hard and long into the whistle. At the very instant she heard the shrill note, Mary felt stung by the realization that she would be leaving! She couldn't leave Hester! *Oh,*

God, it was too late as her world began to disappear in the heat and fatigue. Yes, she could move her arms and legs now, bend at the waist, open her eyes. Mary stared at the bathmat. "I've left the baby on the porch," she whispered.

Chapter Twenty-Six

There was a knock on the bathroom door.

"We've been talking to Mother on the phone, and she's coming down Friday," said Hester.

"Vera's coming?" asked Mary as she opened the door.

"Vera?" said Aunt Hester. "Good gracious, child!" She took Mary's hands in hers. "Vera died years ago. Your Aunt Mary's coming. She's Vera's sister, but she raised me. I don't remember my real mother at all. So I call her my mother. Do you understand? Mary is who I refer to as my mother."

Mary felt faint. "Dead?"

"You don't look well. Do you feel all right?" Hester put her hand on Mary's forehead. "You're warm. I think you should lie down. Finish washing up and I'll turn down the bed."

Dead! God, no! She can't be dead! Please, oh God. Not Vera. No! Mary pulled the whistle from her pocket, sat on the floor and blew it in a fury. This time the journey was welcome. Mary craved the cycling down. She pulled her arms in to quicken it, loath to fight against it. Mary let sensation flee her body as her heart quickened, then eased as she blended with the other body. This time, there was no peaceful arrival.

Mary felt the wind and rain on her face—and the sting of Vera's death.

She gathered up her skirts, raced up the muddy hill to the church and tried the door. By now her hair was slick against her head from the downpour. Her forehead felt numb. Her dress was pasted to her legs. Nell stood beside Mary, panting, oblivious to the storm.

The door was locked, but through the window Mary saw Father hunched over his small desk, writing.

Rain washed down the windowpanes and dripped onto the muddy earth below. Mary tapped on the glass, then rapped with her fist, fearing the glass would shatter but desperate to reach her father. He didn't move except to slip the paper on which he wrote inside the pages of his cherished family Bible. Then he slid the book under his sweater, against his chest.

Mary was moving from the window to the door, when he burst through it, leaving it open to the elements instead of methodically locking it and checking it twice as he'd always done. His sorrowful eyes met Mary's for a brief moment, before he grasped at the Bible concealed under his sweater and started toward the house.

Mary trailed him, Nell following. "You're not the only one who's hurting!" she yelled. "Mother's lost her child, James has lost his wife, and I've lost my *sister!*"

Father turned for an instant to his daughter. "Where's Humphrey?"

Mary stared at the raindrops dripping from his head, over his bony cheeks and nose. Pale and thin, he seemed a ghost hunched before her, squinting and asking, "Where is your brother?"

Then Father fell. He gripped his chest, wilted to the ground and lay bent.

"God forgive me," he whispered.

"It's not your fault," gasped Mary. "You're just worn out, Father."

"Forgive Humphrey," he mumbled. "The letter . . ."

Mary turned toward the house and screamed, "Humphrey! *Help me!*" Her voice quivered with the effort. "*Humphrey!*"

Humphrey sprang from the house and ran toward them. "*Father!* What's happened?" He picked the old man up in his arms, staggering, then catching his balance and walking, weaving to the house. The door was open as Humphrey had left it in his rush, and so he laid his father on his own bed, nearest the door.

Father's eyes closed. "Vera dying." He pinched his lips together as if to summon energy. "My doing."

"No! Not *you!*" said Humphrey, breathing heavily now with the strain of it. "It's all my doing, all my fault."

Father's eyes closed and he opened his mouth to speak but couldn't manage it. His lips were so pale that his mouth looked like an empty hole.

"It's not anyone's fault," said Mary as she rushed alongside. "It's just a dreadful thing that's happened."

As Father's eyes fluttered open, he struggled to retrieve the dog whistle from his pocket.

Humphrey shot a quick look at Mary. "I'm going to get Dr. Cathcart." And then he was gone.

The old man, sallow and weak, pushed the Bible and whistle in Mary's direction. Although no sound came from him, he mouthed, "Humphrey," and Mary understood.

She set them aside, swallowed hard and tried to make her father more comfortable. "To everything there is a season, and a time to every purpose under the heaven. That's what you always say, isn't it? A time to be born and a time to die. A time to mourn and a time to dance. So this is our time to mourn, Father. For Vera." Mary spoke frantically now, as if the pace could keep him breathing.

But when she looked at her father again, his face held an entirely different expression. It was not of pain, because that had ended. But neither was it of peace. Mary searched frantically for a pulse, though she knew in her heart that none would be found.

Mary's face twisted into agonized sobs, disbelieving that this was the way of life, that it was entirely possible to lose someone you love so easily and so quickly and without a proper goodbye. There was not a prayer in the world that could return Vera and Father to her. Life was *not* fair. She'd kept her end of the bargain, caring for Hester as a mother would. But she felt there'd be no reward for her efforts. Mary rested her head on the bed beside her father. Tears streamed down her face and seeped into the wool blanket.

Father's funeral was confusing for her. She couldn't bear being polite and straight-backed for a minute longer. She couldn't hear one more person say that it was a dreadful shock, and ask Mother how she'd manage with the children. How could Mother have a game plan for such a cruel turn of fate?

Mary found Humphrey had fled also, sitting on the barn floor, his head in his hands.

"If I hadn't lost that money," he sobbed uncontrollably now, "we could've afforded better care for Vera and she'd be alive. None of this would've happened. Father's heart was weakened with worry, and then when Vera died, it was just too much."

Mary had placed the whistle and the family Bible on the straw beside her. She picked it up now and handed it to Humphrey.

"Father wanted you to have these," she said.

"I don't deserve the Bible," Humphrey wailed. "I deserve to be dead, in Vera's place, or in Father's place. The money was entrusted to me, it was their first great earning, their salvation in the event of . . ." Humphrey clasped the hair on his head. "I've ruined everything! God knows I didn't mean to . . . I just don't know how it happened . . . but it might have saved her . . . she might've lived if it hadn't been for me."

Mary wrapped her arms around Humphrey. "No one finds you at fault, Humphrey. Why do you keep blaming yourself?" She picked up the Bible again. "Come on," she urged. "Father can't possibly have blamed you or he wouldn't have given you such a treasured possession."

Humphrey took out a handkerchief and blew his nose. His voice was steady now. "He probably wanted me to learn from it."

"Nonsense."

As Mary passed her father's Bible and old dog whistle into her brother's outstretched hands, a powerful feeling overcame her. She suddenly knew who she was and in exactly which time she existed. When she looked at Humphrey's disconsolate face, she no longer saw her brother. He was Grandad, young and heartbroken. It was as though she were watching a movie in which these tragic events were not of her own life, but rather of generations before hers had even begun. She felt empathy for Grandad now, but the deep and bitter sorrow she had felt only minutes before was gone.

Mary knew she had been visiting the past, and the whistle was no longer hers to use. She would never again visit Bircher, never know Grandad as he became a man and his sisters became women. The family would be dispersed like dandelion seeds— each putting down roots in a different place. Mary had been granted a snapshot of family history, and she felt deeply grateful.

Humphrey took the Bible from her and she relinquished the whistle, wrapping her arms around him.

"It'll be all right." She rubbed her hand around and around, making circles on his back, closing her eyes to this tragedy forever. "It's not your fault."

Mary closed her eyes as she held him. In the darkness, she could see the other body splitting from her and spinning slowly away, shrinking in the distance until it was like a snowflake in the night. The cool cloth on her forehead felt good.

"There now, dear," said Aunt Hester as she rinsed and wrung out the facecloth. "It took two of us old-timers just to get you onto your bed! Do us the favor of staying in it for a while until you get your sea legs back."

Those two faces, Grandad's and Aunt Hester's, stared at Mary as they sat perched like tousled owls on the edge of Aunt Hester's bed. The souls she knew so well and loved so much. The nappers. Thank God they were still alive.

Chapter Twenty-Seven

Mary rubbed her eyes and edged onto her elbows. "I feel really confused."

"It's really rather straightforward once you've got everyone figured out," said Aunt Hester.

"I had four sisters, one older and three younger," Grandad began.

Hester looked sidelong at her uncle. "The oldest sister, who was your great Aunt Vera, died of tuberculosis when she was quite young. I was still a baby, really. Vera's younger sister Mary, my aunt, cared for me when Vera died. She'd promised Vera that she'd take care of me, no matter what, and she kept her word."

Mary knew this well. She could almost feel Vera's thin hand when she last held it, the worry on her face, the courage in her letters. Mary could smell the little cottage, the cedar and pine, the smoking fire and stiff towels dried outside on the porch. She'd seen this world. She'd been to Bircher. She knew the burden of responsibility, the swift journey from childhood to adulthood that happens the moment one is entrusted with the raising of a child.

Mary nodded. "Did Aunt Mary marry James?"

"Goodness, no," said Hester. "James loved only Vera. But he loved your Aunt Mary like a sister, and they cared for each other and for me. It was wonderful, really. Just like a mum and dad. I didn't know anything different.

"But what was really awful, as if Vera's dying wasn't enough, is that your great grandfather—that's your Grandad's dad, died shortly after. He had a heart attack, or so the doctor thought at the time. I gather he was dead quite quickly."

"Very quickly," Mary said without thinking. She glanced down to avoid their faces.

The floor creaked and Jester appeared on the landing, just outside the door. He hung his head and tail lower than his barrel-round body and looked at the assembled group on the twin beds.

Grandad gave a sort of growl, as he was inclined to do for disciplinary purposes. But rather than retreating back down the stairs, Jester simply lowered himself onto the soft carpet. Grandad raised his eyebrows and looked slightly embarrassed as his dog continued to disobey him.

"That's my fault, Grandad," said Mary sheepishly. "I sort of . . . I mean I let him . . . sometimes I played . . ."

Grandad looked over the top of his spectacles at his stammering granddaughter. "You let Jester upstairs."

"Yes."

"And up on the bed?"

"Yes."

Grandad's eyebrows lifted again and he twitched his mustache. "Come!" he commanded.

Jester launched himself onto Mary's bed and stretched his sizable body alongside the length of her.

Aunt Hester peeled with laughter.

"Good God!" said Grandad, but made no effort to remove the dog.

"Is it okay?" asked Mary. "Or should I shove him off?"

Grandad looked impish. "Just for tonight."

"Thanks," said Mary, wrapping her arms around Jester. "Now can you tell me the rest of the story?"

Aunt Hester continued. "Now, Grandad's mother was a widow with four remaining children, so she lived in Victoria for a short while, but eventually returned to England with your great aunts Rachael and Eleanor."

"What about you?" Mary asked Grandad.

"I wanted to stay in Victoria where I could finish my schooling and earn a good wage. Mostly, I wanted to help James and Mary with Hester and it seemed the best I could do was send money to them and visit when I could."

"Which was often," smiled Hester.

"Didn't you miss your mum?" asked Mary. "And your sisters?"

Grandad looked at the floor. "I did," he said. "But I felt . . . I just felt that I might . . ."

"Help us out, I think," finished Hester.

There was silence and all three seemed comfortable in it, each sorting out the story, remembering the children they'd once been. Even Mary thought back on her last visit to this house, and how she'd raced about it, oblivious to the inner lives of those around her.

Grandad straightened his spine, then stood and left the room quietly. "It's getting on," he said. "Time for shut-eye."

Before he'd gone out the door, Mary asked, "Would you help me with a family tree before I go home, Grandad? So I can keep it all straight in my mind?"

He turned with a sad expression that Mary found eerily familiar.

"Of course," he said. Then he hobbled out the door.

Aunt Hester leaned toward Mary and whispered, "I'm afraid the story doesn't end there, exactly."

Mary nodded.

"Your poor grandfather feels partly to blame for Vera's death—crazy really. Totally unfounded. But people get ideas in their heads and they grow and fester and stay for such a long time in one's thoughts that they become reality. People were dropping like flies from TB in those days. It could've happened to any of us." Aunt Hester blew her nose with a cotton handkerchief. "I want you to rest now, dear."

Mary pulled the covers up under her chin and closed her eyes. When she did, she could see the image of Humphrey in the barn, his head bowed in anguish, his nose running and tears streaming down his face. It didn't seem fair.

When Mary awoke in the morning, she had the odd feeling that she'd stayed in the very same position for the entire night, so heavy was her sleep. She could hear the rain and a *drip drip drip* from the gutter below the window.

Then she heard the gentle padding of Jester's paws on the stairs and his cautious entry into the guest room.

"Where is everyone?" asked Mary, glancing at the bed beside hers.

They went downstairs together and found no one about. Mary called quietly, wondering if Grandad was perhaps still asleep. But there was no response except the crackling of wood from the fireplace. Someone must be up, she thought.

Perhaps Aunt Hester had dashed to the store for milk. But the grandfather clock ticked the time away in the hall, and still no one appeared.

Finally, Mary threw her Grandad's large raincoat over top of her pajamas and slid on her shoes. Jester sat on the doormat. It was pouring now, and Mary wondered whether she shouldn't just slip back inside and wait. As she dithered in the doorway, she heard the sound of a boat scraping over the rocks on the beach.

"We almost lost the rowboat!" Aunt Hester yelled, the wind stealing her voice. She emerged from the steps to the beach, her hair swirling about.

"Can I help?" The wind blew her hood off and she pulled it back on.

"I've got it now," said Aunt Hester. "Let's go in . . . I've a fire going, it was so cold this morning in the house and I can't bear to turn the heat on in the summer. The wind seemed to be getting through the windows. I thought Tofino was bad!"

Together they trudged up the winding path to the house. Mary followed Aunt Hester. But just as her aunt passed Grandad's den window, a light went on inside. Mary stopped and looked in. It was hard to see clearly, as the wind from the southeast was driving the rain against the window and dripping onto the muddy flowerbed below. Grandad was hunched over his desk, writing. She watched him for a moment, Jester barked impatiently and so Mary could no longer be anonymous. She rapped on the window with her knuckle and Grandad turned his face to Mary.

Their eyes met. Mary's mouth fell open. She looked from his face to his desk to the fountain pen in his hand. Her mind flashed back to Great Grandfather hunched over his small desk in the church, writing furiously. It was as though he had a mission, and Mary's incessant knocking on the window wouldn't deter him. He'd ignored her. He'd just slipped the paper on which he wrote into the Bible before bracing it against his chest and lurching out the door into the driving rain. What was so important about that paper, about what he had written on it? He'd put it in the Bible and he'd wanted Humphrey to have it. But she'd never *told* Humphrey about the paper! And perhaps, in the young boy's grief, he'd never looked inside the Bible. Why would he?

"Was this the reason . . . ?" Mary whispered, "Is this why I went back?"

But the face looking at her was not the grieving face of her great grandfather, panicked and stricken, long fingers quivering. It was Grandad, who had not inherited his own father's aloofness. He smiled at Mary and this shocked her, since she half expected his face to be that of Rudyard Mills. She gasped.

"Oh, my *God!*" Mary yelled, staring in on him, desperately wanting the pieces to fall into place.

Grandad put his hand behind his ear to cock it forward, sensing by her expression that what she had to say was urgent.

Mary raced to catch up to Aunt Hester. Her breathing was heavy. Jester trailed her into the kitchen, as if this sudden burst of speed was a game.

"Mary!" Aunt Hester exclaimed. "Clean off his paws before he comes in the house!"

But Mary only slid off her own shoes, then charged to her Grandad's den. She stopped at the door and held the wood frame with her hands, like a huge spider in the center of a web. Rain dripped onto the rug.

"What the devil are you doing?" asked Grandad.

"I need to see your Bible."

Grandad rose from his chair, leaving the carefully written family tree on the desk. "What for?"

"Where is it?" She let go the door jam, took a few steps into the den and scanned the bookcase.

"Settle down," scolded Grandad. "I don't know what's the matter with you, but you're ruining the carpets. Kindly get your wet things off before you go rifling around in my bookcases."

They stared at each other, their faces a perfect blend of confrontation and bewilderment.

Grandad spoke first. "*I'll* get the Bible." Then he reached up to the topmost shelf of his bookcase and picked off a white, leather-bound Bible. He handed it to Mary, who looked at it incredulously. Something was wrong.

She cracked it open and stared at the type, turned the page. Then she turned to the front inside cover.

"Who's Frances Wright?" she said, pressing now to piece it all together. "Whose Bible is this?"

"Mine."

"Then who's Frances Wright?" Mary repeated, almost yelling now.

Aunt Hester stood at the door. "Are you running a fever, my dear?"

"*Who is Frances Wright? Whose Bible is this?*"

Grandad shot a look of concern at Aunt Hester, who put an arm around Mary.

"Now, dear," she said calmly. "I think it best . . ."

Mary pulled away. "I just want to know who Frances Wright is . . . can you tell me that, *please?*"

Grandad cleared his throat. "Frances Wright was your grandmother's father, and this was his Bible. Now that your grandmother is dead, naturally the Bible is mine. Do you have any more questions?"

"I want to see the Bible that *your* father gave to *you.*"

"But how did you . . . ?" His voice became suddenly quiet, "I know the Bible you're talking about, but I . . ." He trailed off. "I . . . I suspect you . . . how did you . . . ?"

Grandad made his way to the tiny storage cellar under the front hall stairs. Aunt Hester and Mary followed. When he'd opened the door and pulled on the light, he stooped low to stare at the labeled cardboard boxes. *China. Photographs 1945-55. Slides. Fragile Angels. Dressage Equip. Humphrey's Youth.* Mary recognized her grandmother's handwriting.

"Please don't, uncle," said Aunt Hester. "Let me. Is it the one labeled *Humphrey's Youth*?"

Aunt Hester's question went unanswered as she and Mary watched Grandad, bent now to retrieve the box. Mary spoke to the back of his head. "So you've never *looked* at that Bible, never *read* it?"

"It was my father's."

"Yes, I . . ." Mary stopped herself.

"You what?" Grandad slid out the box and pulled open the folded top.

The three of them stood around it as if it was a fire throwing heat. But all that really held their focus was a flimsy piece of plastic encasing a christening gown, folded so that the smocking showed. Aunt Hester gently lifted a corner to reveal a blue wool blanket wrapped also in very thin plastic.

But now Mary grew impatient with their slow dissection of history and plunged her hand into the box. Out came the christening gown and blanket. Then Mary saw the Bible. The vision so hit her that she was suddenly afraid to touch the book as she wondered whether it possessed the magic that the whistle did.

"Is this all about the family tree, Mary? Do you want me to write your name in *this* particular Bible?" Grandad asked patiently.

Mary was thrilled that he'd suddenly given reason for her actions. "Yes!"

Grandad picked up the Bible and read, "Hester Vera Louise Robinson, b.1913 . . ." He looked up and Hester smiled.

"That's where the recording ends," he said, running his long fingers over the script. He looked at Mary. "I'll bring it up to date before you go home."

"But are you *sure* this is the one?" asked Mary. "Are you *sure* it was your father's Bible?"

"Yes," he looked at her over his bifocals. "He was your great grandfather. Rudyard."

"That's the one!" said Mary. "Reverend Rudyard Mills, right?"

"Right."

"And this is the Bible he gave you?"

"Yes."

"For *sure?*"

"In God's name, Mary, *Yes!*" He turned to the very first page and held the book for Mary to see. "Rudyard Carlyon Mills, Beddington Rectory," he read.

Mary eased it out of his hands and began to turn the pages, searching, until finally she found it. A piece of paper.

"What's that?" asked Grandad.

They huddled around it.

"A letter, I think," said Aunt Hester. "Penned in ink."

"My dearest Humphrey," Mary read. She looked at her grandfather, then pressed on. "These words are unbearable . . ." Mary stopped. She handed him the paper.

Grandad took it from her and silently read. As he read, there was a transformation in his face. The corners of his mouth turned down and his eyes grew wide. Deep and way far down in the blueness of them sprang a look of unstoppable grief. Mary immediately felt as if this had all gone very wrong.

"Oh, Grandad, what have I done! I'm so sorry. I just . . . I thought that . . ." her lip quivered. She couldn't believe she was causing such sadness, and after all he'd been through.

"No, no, dear Mary, you can't imagine the good you've done." He paused and looked back down at the letter. "You just can't imagine . . ."

"But . . . ?"

Grandad took a deep breath. "But first I must explain that there was money once, James's money, and I presumed I lost it many years ago. But it seems I didn't lose it at all. Unbelievably, it was your . . ."

He paused for a moment, then handed the paper to Hester. "Read it."

Hester read:

My Dearest Humphrey,

These words are unbearable to write, let alone to think.

I've done you a dreadful injustice, and for a man in my position it is grave indeed. First, I must tell you that it was I who took the money from your school bag. I'd encountered the Mayor earlier in the day and he had informed me of James's good fortune, and I'd further learned that you would be retrieving the money. It was almost the perfect sum to repay a debt I owed my former rectory in England.

The creditors were upon me and I feared for our property. I feared for our family. I became a horse with blinders and my good sense escaped me. James had taken advantage of my dearest Vera and so he should be punished, I conceived, and I imagined I was seeking revenge on James. Little did I realize that I was simply selfish, and that my justification for what amounts to theft would have such far-reaching consequences for myself, for James and Vera, Mother, the girls and you, dear boy.

The worst part of it all is that you, poor lad, have taken the blame for my misdemeanor. Worse still is that our darling Vera would perhaps be alive today if we had had the money for private nursing care. I don't know how many times in my life that I've preached about just one action affecting many. Now look at me. You have a coward for a father.

We might surely be living as we did in England, with all the comforts afforded us had I not mismanaged the rectory's finances. It was Grandmama who financed our passage to Canada, the purchase of our land, our very survival. With her meager pension, we were safe from the social humiliation. Yet it is far worse, I now know, to be humiliated in your soul. We are all penniless now, and without one of our dearest.

I don't know how to free myself from the inner pain I feel. I've turned to God and He has told me to begin with this letter. I want to free you before I decide how to approach Mother, Mary, and James. You've suffered as a consequence of my sins. And you are truly a son who makes his father very proud.

I beg you to forgive me.

Father

Grandad cupped his face in one hand and was silent. Aunt Hester put her arms around his shoulders. This was good, Mary thought as she stood alone in the middle of the hallway. Mum had always told her that it was good and cleansing and helpful to cry. These were tears of resolution.

Mary felt it was time to leave the others alone. She tiptoed up the stairs and ran a bath. She felt chilled to the bone. Her hair was wet and her teeth chattered. When she finally slipped in, she stayed for a long time, adding more hot water and staring blankly at the islands of her knees. There was much to digest and much she didn't understand about her recent and magical acquisition of family history.

When the soles of her feet were prunish, Mary rose from the tub and dressed. Jester's tail thumped on the carpeting as she descended the stairs. Mary stopped on the landing and looked again at the portrait of Rudyard Mills. The colors were somewhat subdued, except the apricot accents in his face. Mary didn't feel the warmth from the portrait as she had before, and wondered if it had been the fever that had altered her judgement. Even the eyes were less intense, though the expression appeared as if he might at any moment engage in conversation. "Maybe you're not just a painting," she whispered, as she ran her finger along the frame.

Mary didn't find Grandad and Hester in the dining room as usual, but instead heard them talking quietly in the living room.

"It's as though Father's hand was guiding Mary," said Grandad.

"Isn't it?" Hester agreed. "It's very strange."

"It's as if the old man was sorting things out, through *her*."

Mary stepped into the room and sat in one of the big chairs.

Grandad smiled at her. "Mary, there's something I want to ask you."

"What?"

"I . . ." The old man put his weathered hand on the dog's head.

"What?"

"How did you know about the Bible?"

Looking down at the floor, Mary struggled for an explanation. She didn't understand it herself, how could she explain it to Grandad? *I time-traveled . . . I was your sister in 1913 . . . I dreamed it . . .*

Mary held her breath, hoping to somehow articulate her experience, the way grown ups do. Maybe he could read her mind . . . stranger things had happened in this house. So she chose to answer honestly, though not completely. "I don't really know."

Grandad looked at her over his bifocals, his expression neutral. His blue eyes seemed to penetrate hers. Then he spoke. "Your grandmother saw a ghost once, you know."

"Mum told me. In England, right?"

He nodded. "Yes, in England."

"I heard that story," Hester chimed in.

Grandad crossed his legs. "Do you believe in ghosts, Mary?"

She looked at him now, feeling a curious sense of confidence. "Yes, I think I do."

Mary saw a hint of a smile, of release perhaps, in Grandad's eyes. She guessed that her answer was enough. His calm gave her the courage to bring up a subject that had been on her mind for a long time.

"I guess it wouldn't hurt to hang that portrait now, eh, Grandad?"

The old man raised his eyebrows. "It wouldn't hurt at all." He smiled.

She recognized the twinkle in his eye from so many years ago. She remembered how kindly he was with the new calf, the puppy Isobel, and baby Hester. Mary loved him for his compassion and goodness, his sense of right and wrong.

His own father's mistakes in life had altered the course of the entire family. Yet Rudyard Mills had intended to make right his mistake, in the eyes of his family, and of his God. Now it was done. Late, but never is it too late.

About the Author

As a third generation Vancouverite, Valerie Rolfe Lupini fled the big city twelve years ago to raise her family on Bowen and Vancouver islands. After the birth of her second son came the publication of her first book, *There Goes the Neighbourhood,* followed by a decade of mothering and homeschooling. Now that her sons are older, she's found time to write again. *The Whistle,* though clearly fiction, developed after she delved into her family's colorful homesteading history.